"You're not here to tell me how to live my life," Jake growled.

"I'm trying to help you." Angelica laid a hesitant hand on his arm. "Moreover, I'm trying to help myself. You give me the impression you think I'm the sort of woman who might hurt you."

She was so beautiful, with that abundant hair flowing around her face, and her eyes as dark as night. He wanted to kiss her, deeply, lavishly, with all the passion that beat in his blood.

"I never believed in a witch until I met you," he said, wondering what it would be like to keep her forever.

"Yet you still call me Angel? I have to tell you that no one else has called me that." It seemed important to bring that fact to his attention. "You need to think about that, Jake McCord. Because I can't be both...."

Margaret Way takes great pleasure in her work and works hard at her pleasure. She enjoys tearing off to the beach with her family at weekends, loves haunting galleries and auctions and is completely given over to French champagne "for every possible joyous occasion." She was born and educated in the river city of Brisbane, Australia, and now lives within sight and sound of beautiful Moreton Bay.

Books by Margaret Way

HARLEQUIN ROMANCE®
3595—A WIFE AT KIMBARA*
3607—THE BRIDESMAID'S WEDDING*
3619—THE ENGLISH BRIDE*
3664—GENNI'S DILEMMA
     (part of HUSBANDS OF THE OUTBACK, with Barbara Hannay)
3671—MASTER OF MARAMBA
3679—OUTBACK FIRE
3707—STRATEGY FOR MARRIAGE
3715—MISTAKEN MISTRESS

*LEGENDS OF THE OUTBACK

HARLEQUIN SUPERROMANCE®
762—THE AUSTRALIAN HEIRESS
966—THE CATTLE BARON
1039—SECRETS OF THE OUTBACK

MARGARET WAY

Outback Angel

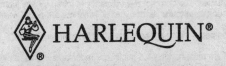

TORONTO • NEW YORK • LONDON
AMSTERDAM • PARIS • SYDNEY • HAMBURG
STOCKHOLM • ATHENS • TOKYO • MILAN • MADRID
PRAGUE • WARSAW • BUDAPEST • AUCKLAND

ISBN 0-373-03727-9

OUTBACK ANGEL

First North American Publication 2002.

Visit us at www.eHarlequin.com

Printed in U.S.A.

CHAPTER ONE

THE heat and clamour of the day had been frightful, Jake reflected. Truly exhausting even for him. It had been easy enough rounding up the mob on the spinifex plains at the height of the Dry, fields of burnt gold like an endless harvest of wheat, but galloping after cattle in rough terrain was no fun. And dangerous.

Last year his Brit jackeroo, Charlie Middleton, had sustained a back injury as a result of his boundless derring-do and yen for action and had to undergo surgery, which mercifully turned out fine. Charlie, the Honourable Charles Middleton, no less, was back on the job a whole lot less inclined to go swashbuckling around the bush. He really liked Charlie and mostly looked on his enthusiasm and sense of adventure with favour, but the ever-present hazards had to be taken seriously. Driving cleanskins, the unbranded cattle, out of their hiding places was one of them. The horned beasts, dangerous on that count alone, buried themselves deep in the vast network of lignum thickets that wrapped themselves around the waterways and billabongs, finding green havens after the semidesert with its scorching red sands.

This was the final muster before Christmas. The Big One, though work procedures had been revolutionised since he was a boy. Today on the station good chopper pilots—and he was one of them—matched the skills of the pioneer stockmen when it came to moving cattle. The name of the game was efficiency and the use of helicopters had greatly increased the speed of the musters as well as cutting the workforce. But there were some places the choppers couldn't safely go, so the horses got involved, every last one of them well trained. That was his job. Overseeing their management.

A man had to be multi-skilled these days to survive on the land. He was a smart businessman, too. He had a degree in commerce behind him. A man for all seasons you might say.

And speaking of seasons, the Wet had officially begun in the tropical north of his giant state of Queensland, but not one drop of rain had fallen on his neck of the woods; the far south-west of the state, the Channel Country, riverine desert with some of the loneliest, most dramatic landscapes on the planet. Home to the nation's cattle kings. He guessed he had to be one of them now.

Jake McCord. Cattle king. Jake was grittier than Jonathon, his real name. Of course his father had come up with the alternative. He supposed it was reasonably close. Only his mother had called him Jonathon. Three years after his father's premature death—Clive McCord had been bitten in the leg by a poisonous copperhead while out on one of his solitary desert walkabouts—he still thought of himself as the heir apparent. The man in waiting. He supposed it was to his credit he had never thought of himself as being overshadowed by his father when his father had clearly enjoyed cracking the whip as a means of keeping everyone around him under control.

Especially his son. However, in his case, his father had never tasted success. Some inbred fighting spirit had allowed him to shrug and take it. He knew a lot of people in their far-flung Outback community put the discord between father and son down to Clive McCord's not unrare jealousy of his heir and his deep-seated bitterness. The fact was, both of their lives had been tragically disrupted by the death of beautiful, much loved, Roxanne, wife and mother, in a riding accident on the station when Jake was barely six. From then on his father had turned into another person, with hardly a nodding tolerance for others, not drawing closer to his bereft child, but seeming to blame him for living when his wife hadn't. There was ample proof that sort of thing sometimes happened.

The total lack of love and approval had left him damaged

he supposed. It had certainly charged him with a lot of hurt and anger and an almost chronic wariness that even extended into his love life. He supposed it was all about his mother and his idealisation of her. It had been very hard on his girl-friends because one way or another they had all fallen short. Or perhaps he believed that love was an illusion. Yet he had known love when his mother was alive. He was still capable of remembering. Her loss had been overwhelming and it had come at a bad time in a child's life.

Two years after his mother's death, Stacy had come along. Stacy, his stepmother, his father's second wife. Poor Stacy! God what a life she'd had with such a hard strange man who'd only married her because she was nothing like his late wife, but she was young, gentle and tractable and could provide from her delicate body more sons to work the giant station. All Stacy could manage was his half sister, Gillian, who had proved as easy to dominate as her mother, flinching whenever her father's hard gaze fell on her. It would have been easier for Gillian had she been a McCabe in appearance. His clan tended to be really handsome people with a surplus of self-confidence. Gillian favoured her mother. Pretty, sure, but living life under a modern-day despot who never saw her as any kind of asset had clipped Gilly's wings. Sometimes he thought it hadn't helped anyone when he'd come so repeatedly to their defence. It had only made his father look more harshly on all of them.

McCord's sudden violent death was an appalling shock when they all thought he was going to live forever, but in the end he hadn't been mourned. Stacy and Gillian had made a pretence at grief—surely it was expected—but it wasn't in Jake to play the hypocrite. All of them after the initial shock had felt a vast sense of release. For such a rich and powerful man, his father had had few genuine friends except for an old aboriginal called Jindii, an Eaglehawk man, who sometimes joined McCord on his wanderings. Jindii, a desert nomad, had passed back and forth across the station for as long as anyone could remember. In fact the old man had to be at

least one hundred and looked every minute of it. Jindii still
wandered the Wild Heart. So did his father for that matter.
In spirit anyway. He had scattered his father's ashes in a
high-noon ritual, watching them disappear in a sea of mirage
to become part of the eternal shifting sands.

So now he was McCord, the master of Coori Downs. Coori
was an aboriginal word meaning flowers. And vast vistas of
desert flora was what the first Scottish-born McCord settler
in Australia had seen when he and an explorer friend had
passed through the Channel Country on their journey to the
Central Queensland plains in the early 1800s. Jake had whole
sections of his ancestor's diaries off pat....

"Wildflowers marching to the horizons!" His ancestor had
written. "Mile after mile of them, as far as a man can see.
A sight that gave me a sense of God; of great kinship with
this ancient earth. Under those infinite desert gardens, surely
the mightiest on earth, lay the bones of the explorers who
had perished. Men like Kingsley and me. Ordinary men but
adventurers, too. Men of vision. It seemed impossible such
displays could exist under the blazing sun. There were countless millions of daisies with white and gold petals like paper.
Pink succulents, yellow poppies, delicate, fragrant indigo,
purple, brilliant red bushes that looked like they'd caught fire.
And grasses of lilac, silver and pale green were waving their
feathery plumes before the wind. A wonderful, wonderful
sight, breath-taking in its unexpectedness. It was like entering
Paradise after the savagery of the country through which we
had passed, harsh and unforgiving enough to break a man's
spirit. The temptation to stay in this flowering wilderness was
enormous but Kingsley rightly reminded me we had to meet
up with the main party at an isolated settlement eight days
hence."

His intrepid ancestor had returned ten years later, to almost
the exact spot, this time with his family, his wife and four
sons, to lay the foundation for the McCord dynasty. It had
proved a hard life with undreamed-of tribulations, but the

family had survived and triumphed. The days of the pioneers had been meticulously recorded in several diaries.

It was a harsh code Jake had lived under himself. Not materially, the reputed family wealth was no fiction. His father deserved respect for the management of his heritage. Coori had prospered under his stewardship, but somehow from a twisted soul his father had set about trying to deplete his only son's resources. But in the best tradition of his forefathers, it had only made Jake tougher. Survival of the fittest was the name of the game. A man still had to contend with the rules of the jungle.

As for Stacy? She hadn't had much of a life. Married off at eighteen to a man of difficult character almost twenty years her senior. Just to add to it, Stacy had to live with the fact she was in a triangular marriage, even if her rival was a tragic ghost, the memory of his mother, Roxanne.

Her portrait had never come down. It continued to hang above the mantelpiece in the Yellow Drawing Room. A study of a beautiful young woman on the eve of her marriage to one of the most eligible young men in the country, Clive McCord of the McCord pioneering dynasty. He tried to remember his father as a young man. Certainly his early childhood memories had been filled with happy times. Enough to sustain him.

But the young Clive McCord had all but disappeared the day they brought his wife in on a stretcher, slender neck broken in a fall from her beloved Arabian mare, Habibah, though she'd been an experienced horsewoman. His father had shot Habibah where it stood, sweating and trembling. Jake remembered that bright, shining, beautiful animal crashing to the ground as vividly as though it were yesterday. He remembered his screams of protest, rushing to his father, grasping him around the legs in an effort to divert his aim. Habibah was his mother's horse. She would never have wanted it destroyed. It was an accident, but it may as well have been murder so far as his father was concerned. Despite the agony of his son, Clive McCord had pulled the trigger, his insides burning with grief and rage.

I've such a memory, he thought, feeling a moment of depression, it burdens me. He stopped on his journey from the stables to the house to eye a falcon about to drop on its prey. He clapped his hands, looking skyward at the blazing desert sunset.

"Scat!" Immediately the falcon flew off with a sharp, predatory and mournful cry that startled the family cat, Tosca, who had the same colouring as Jake. It amused him, though Stacy always said he was more like a lion. He bent to the cat, as it purred in contentment and wound itself around his leg, stroking and murmuring a few endearments that Tosca seemed to enjoy. He loved all animals though he'd had his arguments with wild camels and dingoes. He loved horses especially, it was a love born and bred in him. Horses were essential to his unique way of life. He was highly skilled at educating them and keeping them fit and sound in tough conditions. He couldn't help knowing that he was widely regarded as a superb rider and polo player, as well.

The truly frustrating thing was while he was a damned good judge of a horse's character, he hadn't had such luck with women. One in particular had hurt him, but that was in his university days. Her name was Michelle. She was a few years older, and a smooth, smooth, operator. She played games when one thing he prized in a relationship was trust. And he didn't share. He was still waiting like a fool for that thunderbolt from the heavens, the perfect woman, or perfect for him, and he was twenty-eight years old. A man of strong passions, but he made damn sure they didn't appear too near the surface. How different life would be with that one woman. He still hadn't closed his mind on the idea he would find her. Or she would find him. God knows he had little time to go courting. That was the curse of the man on the land.

He heaved a weary sigh. He found sweet and endearing his stepmother and half sister. He loved them for their gentle caring natures but even at the best of times they weren't women to lean on. They had an excellent housekeeper in Clary. Clary had her own little band of household staff, part aboriginal girls born on the station, gone away to school, but happy to come back. Still, the homestead by any standards was a mansion and Clary wasn't getting any younger. The house girls needed direction. He certainly didn't need Stacy and Gilly to help him run the station and their two out-stations hundreds of miles away in Central Queensland, but it would have been brilliant had they been more confident and competent, able to run things, order up supplies, manage the domestic staff, all the sorts of things women traditionally did on an Outback station.

Like Dinah, for instance. He could just picture Dinah Campbell running the Christmas functions Coori would be hosting this year, although he had given the job to his cousin, Isobel, who ran a very successful catering business for the well-heeled in Brisbane. Even so, Dinah had come close to telling him she would have been just as good at the job, humming softly to herself as she explored all the reception rooms of the house, making suggestions as to what needed changing, a seriously desirous expression in her eyes; laughing right under his nose about Stacy's "problems" until she saw she was making him furious.

Dinah, a genuine platinum-blonde with pale green eyes, was a good-looking, totally capable and assured young woman but her strong point wasn't tact or understanding, maybe you couldn't have one without the other, and he didn't care at all for her patronising his family. He'd known Dinah since they were children. Like him, she was Outback royalty, grand-daughter to his McCord grandfather's closest friend. He had even romanced her on and off. Dinah could be good fun, as well as being good in bed. He knew she valued their long friendship, but there was something about her he couldn't really cotton on to. Could it be her lack of feeling for others? God knows he'd had enough of that, though she was always incredibly sweet to him. He was aware Dinah and her family had high hopes that one day he would "pop the question" though he had never led Dinah to believe it was only a matter of time.

Yes, he could picture Dinah organising everything perfectly, compulsively methodical, looking glamorous while she savoured playing Coori's hostess, circling the guests using all her practised charm, and supreme self-confidence that came with having a rich man for a doting dad. So why had he rejected her? In many ways she had fit the bill. She was strong, with energy to burn. She was Outback born and had lived his way of life. Moreover he needed someone. A woman he could love and live with for the rest of his life. Where the hell was she? If she ever turned up he knew he would recognise her right off.

Some of his more delicious dreams stirred… He kept seeing a pair of dark eyes. A wonderful fall of dark curly hair, glossy as a magpie's wing. Even thinking about it drew all the blood into his loins. But he didn't know a single girl with large lustrous dark eyes and a beautiful soft body that drew a man like a magnet. At one point he thought he had actually seen her someplace. Somewhere outside his dreams. Then he decided she was simply a figment of his imagination.

Stacy was waiting for him the moment he set foot in the homestead. Even after all these years she still had the capacity to surprise him. She was sitting cross-legged on the parqueted floor, flanked by the two coal-black Labradors, Juno and Jupiter, tails thumping in an ecstasy of greeting.

"What on earth are you doing down there?" He braced himself as the dogs bounded towards him.

Stacy smiled sweetly and shrugged. "Why not? It's nice and cool. Besides I've never felt comfortable in those chairs." She nodded at two very imposing and valuable antique carved mahogany hall chairs with sphinx-like figures for arms. At forty Stacy was in great shape. She still looked like a girl, with her fair hair and skin and large cloudy blue eyes. She'd lived a lifetime of constantly trying to please, but somehow she didn't show the burden of endless stress.

Arrested development, one of the acerbic McCord aunts had observed. No one in the extended family could ever work out why the high-handed, difficult and demanding Clive had married such a consistently shy and ineffectual little thing. Stacy wasn't considered interesting or exciting at all. Why, she couldn't be more different to the beautiful, vivid Roxanne whom everyone had adored and greatly mourned.

Now Stacy stood up, swaying a little because she had pins and needles in her left foot, a neat figure in her cotton shirt and jeans, the great crystal waterfall that was the hall chandelier putting highlights into her short cap of fair hair.

"Isobel called," she announced, as though conducting a conversation with his dynamo of a cousin had left her vaguely distraught.

"Oh?" At this time of year Isobel's business was running full-tilt, but she had come to his rescue yet again. Isobel, married to a well-known Federal M.P. was particularly sensitive to his plight. Kinder than most of the McCord clan, even Isobel found Stacy's lack of social and organization skills extremely unfortunate.

"So what did she want?" he prompted as Stacy seemed to have come to the end of her speech.

"Malcolm had a sick turn in the P.M.'s office." She said it like it was the high point of Malcolm's career. "He's going into hospital in the morning so they can run a few tests."

"Oh, Lord, I'll have to call her." He ran a hand through his thick hair, dismayed on two counts. He really liked Malcolm, and this could put paid to the up-coming Coori festivities. "Maybe exhaustion," he mused, hopefully. "Malcolm works harder than most."

"I didn't know any of them really worked," said Stacy who had no insight into a busy politician's life at all. "But I'm sorry about Malcolm. He's one of the few to never be nasty to me. And they're such a compatible couple."

"I guess some marriages have to work out," he offered

distractedly, his mind ticking over. Even his rock-solid cousin would be a mess if anything was really wrong with Malcolm, God forbid. And it would put paid to Isobel's indispensable services. Maybe he would have to turn to Dinah, after all. She'd really love that.

"What if Isobel can't handle our functions?" Stacy asked thoughtfully, not considering for a minute she should have a go. "You might have to fall back on Dinah. I hope you don't have to." She cast him a quick look. "Isobel flusters me, I almost have to run to catch up with her, but Dinah makes me feel an utter fool."

"Why don't you tell her off?" he suggested briskly, no longer embarrassed by his stepmother's inadequacies. "That might give both of you a good shake-up. Eventually, Dinah might even stop."

"But she's your friend!" Stacy stared at him incredulously, as if somehow that gave Dinah free rein. "I'm not game to say a word to her," she confessed, thinking even Dinah's smile had a sneer in it. "I must be such a disappointment to you, Jake." Stacy brushed her wispy fringe from her forehead. "I was certainly cut from a different cloth than the likes of Isobel and Dinah."

Wasn't that the truth! From his childhood his role had been to be supportive of Stacy. Even now Stacy couldn't speak his mother's name, though he had often caught her staring up at Roxanne's portrait. Roxanne, who even as a young bride had handled the role of mistress of a great historic station with brilliant aplomb.

"From all McCord accounts an imbecile." From nowhere tears suddenly rolled down Stacy's cheeks, though he knew from long experience anything could trigger them.

After all these years it didn't break him up. "Cut it out now," he braced her automatically, feeling it would be wise to get Gillian started on some course or other. He didn't want his half sister feeling such confusion about herself and her life. "Organising and running functions isn't the only thing in the world." The Lord is my strength and my shield, he thought wryly. He had been relying on Isobel to get them through.

"I'm really, really sorry, Jake." Stacy's tears stopped on the instant. It was taking time for her to remember with his father gone there was nothing to fear.

"Don't worry, we'll manage," Jake reassured her.

Stacy sighed with relief. Nothing ever rattles him, she thought gratefully, looking up into her stepson's dynamic face. Even terrible things. She supposed that was keeping up the McCord tradition, when the McCord tradition had beaten her down. As often happened, she had the sense of looking at his mother. The beautiful young woman her husband had never forgotten. Jake had the same glorious tawny colouring. The thick, thick, wavy hair, amber, streaked with gold. Roxanne, in the portrait, had great coils of it. Jake's was a lion's mane. They both had amber eyes to match, which were spectacularly beautiful, full of sparkle and life. The passionate nature of mother and son showed in the vitality of their expressions, the cut of the beautifully defined sensuous mouths. Mouths you couldn't look away from. Jake was tall, as had been Roxanne. At six-three, even taller than his father, young-man lean, wide shoulders narrowing to a trim waist, long taut flanks. He was superbly fit from his hard outdoor life. Jake was a wonderful-looking young man, exotic in his tawny splendour. His mother, Roxanne, had been incandescent in her beauty. Even dead, she's more alive than I am, Stacy thought ironically. She was quite quite certain she would never have survived living with Clive McCord if it weren't for his son.

Malcolm as it turned out required surgery. An ultrasound confirmed he would have to have his gall bladder removed. It would be keyhole surgery with a minimum recovery time, but his devoted wife couldn't think of leaving him. Isobel apologised to Jake twice. Jake said not to worry. But even then, worried Isobel took charge. By midmorning of the next day she left a message that she had found someone she thought would be perfect to take over her job. A wonderful young woman she had taken under her wing, with a background in fine food. Her parents owned and ran a prize-winning restaurant. Her protégée was a food writer with the up-market magazine, *Cosima,* sometimes she guested for other highly regarded magazines. She wasn't a chef as such, but a darn good cook—she had helped Isobel with several important functions. Isobel could highly recommend her. The paragon whose name was Angelica De Campo, would ring Jake that very night. If he liked the sound of her, the deal could be stitched up. There was little time to lose.

Jake received all this information when he returned to the homestead at sundown. He started to relax as his worries began to fall off him. Isobel wouldn't recommend anyone she didn't have the utmost faith in. He was at his desk in the study looking over an industry report when Miss De Campo's call came through.

"Mr. McCord?"

Her voice was so mellifluous, so much like honey, he actually slumped back in his leather chair, feeling a delicious lick of it on his tongue. "Miss De Campo. How good of you to call." He on the other hand sounded quite sardonic. Sometimes, he thought ruefully, he even sounded like his father, which really bothered him.

"Isobel will have told you about me?" Honey Throat was asking. Hell, the effect on him was fantastic! He had to control the force of his exhalation.

"The only thing she omitted to do was send a picture. I'm sure, though, you're most attractive." God, he wanted her to be. That voice and good looks. A winning combination! And she could cook, and handle big functions anyplace, even the middle of the Outback. What a joy! He was stunned to think there were women like that out there. Maybe she also had huge dark eyes, and beautiful, womanly breasts. Of course, being a great cook there was more than a slight possibility she could be overweight and sensitive about it. He mustn't place too much importance on a great voice.

"You can decide when you see me," she laughed. "I hope I pass. That's if you want me to take over from Isobel, Mr. McCord. You might like to ask me a few questions?"

"Indeed," he answered, trying and succeeding in sounding the tough businessman. "My first. You've never handled functions of this size by yourself?"

"No, not as big, but that's fine," she returned with pleasing poise. "Size is no problem. I've had a lot of experience in catering to numbers. Isobel would have told you my parents are in the hospitality business. They run an excellent restaurant. I know all their sources, the top people to contact. I've done a lot of P.R. I'm currently working on a pre-Christmas party for Billie Reynolds, the millionaire stockbroker?"

She said it like it was a question and he nearly answered, "Bah!" Shades of his father again. "I do recognise the name." Billie Reynolds fell into the serial-womanising category. Trying to count his ex-wives would be like trying to count sheep. "How do you think it will turn out?"

"Wonderful, even if I say so myself." She sounded convinced. "Billie wouldn't have hired me if I couldn't deliver. He's a perfectionist."

"So you're brilliant then?" he lightly mocked, positive she was.

"I work hard at what I do," she told him modestly. "I've learned a great deal watching my parents and Isobel, of course. I admire her tremendously. She's enormously successful. I was quite upset when I heard about Malcolm."

"Then you'll know his surgeon is speaking about a quick recovery." She had obviously drawn herself into the family circle.

"Yes. Belle and I are constantly in touch."

Well listen to that! Belle. "I gather you're something of a protégée?" Another deadpan delivery. Just like his dear dad.

What if this thing grew and grew? The thought was downright scary.

"Belle is very good at spotting talent."

Was it possible she was having a go at him? He didn't actually mind.

"I'm very flattered she recommended me," she added.

"And I have to say I'm enormously relieved." He whisked away the rest of his Scotch. "At this time of year I'm nearly running on empty. You realise how isolated the station is?" There would be plenty of opportunities for showing her around.

"Isobel has described everything," she answered, totally unfazed. "As I understand it, you'll be hosting the finals of the Marsdon Polo Cup with a luncheon followed by afternoon tea. Finishing up with a gala ball that evening. The following week, there'll be a barbecue for all the staff and their families. And the Saturday before Christmas you're hosting a large party for all your relatives and friends." She sounded like she was ticking them off; she seemed a young woman of considerable competence who could handle things on her own.

Aside from Dinah, who didn't have a voice like strawberry-flavoured brandy, he had never had such an experience.

"Do I have that right?" she asked.

"I should throw in it's my birthday, as well." That might faze her.

"Is it?"

He heard the smile in her voice, resolved to hold on to his cool. "No, but I've waited all my life to have one. A party, that is."

A pause. "That sounds a little sad. But you've got plenty of time."

"How could you know I'm twenty-eight?"

"Isobel must have mentioned it."

"Then you also know I'm a bachelor?" It was perfectly clear they were flirting. Or at least he was. It amazed him. Proof positive he needed a woman clever enough to get under his skin. "My birthday's in August by the way. I'm the definitive Leo."

"That's interesting. So am I. Shall I write a party down under Future Projects?"

He swung around in the swivel chair. "Well, you'd best work for me first, don't you think?"

"Great idea! Say the word and I can start. You won't find me a disappointment."

"How expensive are you, Miss De Campo?" She told him. Wow! Pulling in money like that was something to brag about. On the other hand Isobel, even if she was his cousin, didn't come cheap, either.

"Everything will be the best," she explained. "That means expensive, but I say pay it every time. There's no substitute for quality."

"Sure," he agreed laconically. "You must take your pay home in an armoured van."

"No, but a security guard walks me to my car. Now, why don't we discuss what you plan over Christmas?"

Why not? Maybe by August they'd be married. He let his sense of humour take over. If this woman had beautiful dark eyes he'd fall into her arms. He needed a really great love affair to free him up. It was so long since he'd had one. Hell, he'd never had one. They spoke back and forth for another ten minutes, both adopting a no-nonsense manner as they got down to detail. He asked many more questions of her, she gave all the right answers. Isobel knew her stuff. Miss Angelica De Campo was hired.

After he put the phone down, he leaned back in his chair and closed his eyes. It struck him Miss De Campo's effect on him had been dangerously seductive. Either that or it was the effects of a glancing blow to the head in the scrub.

CHAPTER TWO

JUST over a week later Angelica stepped onto the tarmac of an Outback airport terminal into a shimmering landscape of heat. Waves of it bounded up from the ground at her. For an instant it almost took her breath away, like a sudden blast from an oven, until she decided to confront it head-on, moving her long legs purposefully, eyes straight ahead, not drawing in all the admiring glances, so she was among the first to reach the air-conditioned cool of the terminal building. There she snapped her dark mane of hair back from her heat-pricked forehead. She thought of the challenging weeks ahead of her; the amount of work she had to do even with help.

Isobel had cautioned her about the heat but she didn't quite understand until it hit her. She was thankful for her olive skin and Mediterranean heritage, otherwise she thought her skin might have melted. Not that she wasn't used to heat, living in Brisbane. But there it was the languid golden heat of the tropics, with high humidity. This heat was different. It felt more like a dry bake. Still, it couldn't diminish her excitement about the project.

She was exuberant about the whole thing. She couldn't wait to get to Coori Downs, which she'd heard was remarkable. Isobel had been meaning to show her a magazine which featured quite a spread on the historic homestead but Malcolm's hospitalisation had naturally preoccupied her mind. Pity! There was supposed to be a great shot of the current cattle baron, a man, from all accounts, to turn heads. Promising!

The scope of the functions would establish what she could do, enhancing her career, but she had to say as well as the

Outback venue, she'd been mightily attracted by the prospect of meeting Isobel's cousin, Jake. He'd sounded so sexy over the phone, the memory still made her knees go weak. His father, according to Isobel, had been a regular fire-eater, but the son sounded very easy in his power, as though it fitted him like a great pair of jeans. The nicest, most considerate thing was, he was actually flying in from his desert stronghold to pick her up. She had been expecting to catch a charter flight but it was Jake who suggested he collect her. She loved people who did favours.

In the rest room she freshened up, piling her extravagant mass of hair into a knot of sorts at the back. She had no idea how long it would stay there. Her hair had a mind of its own. For the trip she'd kept her outfit simple. A white sleeveless top in a softly clingy fabric, teamed with her favourite denim mini. It showed yards of leg but she wore it unselfconsciously.

She had learned to take comfort in her jaunty thoroughbred legs even if their length did turn her into a very tall woman. She stood six feet in high heels and she wasn't one for flatties. Her height had made her a basketball star in high school. Even so she never slumped—for that she had to thank her mother who was also tall—and she held her head high even though there were lots of guys who had to look up to her. The man to sweep her off her feet, and she just knew he was out there, would have to be a latter day John Wayne. Despite that, she'd been hotly pursued for years. What did they call her in the columns? The luscious Angelica De Campo. Not that she carried an ounce of fat but she had inherited an eye-catching bust from the Italian side of the family.

Men saw her as a challenge. She remembered one in particular. A married man, a powerful, destructive, merchant banker—she had helped out catering a party for his wife— who simply wouldn't take no for an answer. As he saw it, he could have anyone with his fat wallet. In the end, exercising her discretion—God knows what boundaries her father would have crossed for his "little" girl—she told her brother,

Bruno, who was six-six. Bruno managed to convince the banker to stay away or the outlook would be lousy. She hadn't asked Bruno to explain his methods. Whatever they were, they'd worked. Probably the banker thought Bruno was a paid-up member of the Mafia. Still the experience had left a nasty taste in the mouth.

Certain men could be quite frightening when they developed a fixation on a woman. Mr. Merchant Banker had been one of them, but that was a few years back. She did occasionally agonise over it, if only because she and the banker had been caught out getting physical in a near frenzy of a wrestle, she, even at her superior height fighting hard for her honour. She wished she'd seen that guy again. The one who'd looked at her so contemptuously from his extraordinary lion's eyes. She'd soon put him straight. Only she never laid eyes on him again. Not once during the intervening years and she had to admit she'd never grown tired of looking.

Embarrassments and scandals. She was very careful these days men being what they were. It seemed they only had to look at a well-endowed woman. And she came from a decent, normal, well-adjusted family.

Jake saw her before she saw him. She was staring out the plate-glass window, watching a private jet fly in. Even if the excited female attendant hadn't pointed her out—apparently Miss De Campo had made any number of appearances on television—he'd have picked her. Despite the extreme simplicity of her dress—her skirt seemed to end at her armpits—he couldn't fail to recognise the quality people generally called style. It oozed out of her and he was only looking at her side-on. She looked incredibly sexy in that unique way European women had, she seemed innocently seductive without being sultry, with her lashings of dark, mahogany hair with a decided curl. She had to have dark Italian eyes. She couldn't have looked better had he dreamed her up. He didn't even mind her height, which would have her towering over Stacy and Gillian. She wouldn't tower over him. This was a woman he could meet face-to-face.

"Miss De Campo?"

She reacted instantaneously, as if he had pushed a button, swinging around, a lovely buoyant smile on her face, sparkle of beautiful teeth; a smile that ludicrously…froze.

They stared at one another transfixed. Horror, fascination, disbelief flitted across both their faces. To put it mildly, both were shocked into a near paralysis as they began to track one another down. That party! One of those horribly mortifying incidents that reverberate forever.

She was the last woman in the world he expected. Jake was suddenly, violently, fathoms deep into the past. He felt anger and disappointment along with the most profound scarcely rational disillusionment. After all, she hadn't arrived as his mail-order bride. But over the phone she had intrigued him to the extent he had gone about his work all week with a warm secret feeling lurking in his heart; the idea she just could be the woman to fulfil his dreams. He still believed in the idea. Now all his daydreams had been swept away. Miss Angelica De Campo had a very bad habit. She played erotic games that got out of control. Memory clicked in, all the more mysterious because such picture of her he had, had only lasted a few moments. Afterwards, defiantly he had blocked her out, but other images of her were locked in his subconscious.

This was another one of those woman who drew men like bees. Women like Michelle who these days scarcely seemed to count. Even Michelle had never looked like this! Such women often gave exquisite joy before they delivered the body blows. His big problem was Miss De Campo, like Michelle, didn't adhere to his idea of decent principles. Miss De Campo was a home wrecker. A woman who got an emotional fix out of seducing married men.

It had to be almost three years since he'd attended that party thrown by Trevor and Carly Huntley. He'd had little to do with Huntley, barely making a connection. Trevor Huntley was a wealthy merchant banker, but Carly was a relative. He was in town on business. Carly had run into him coming out of his hotel, expressed her delight and surprise at seeing him, and invited him to their party that night. He'd had nothing else to do, so he'd gone along, waiting until the party was well under way before he made an appearance.

The Huntleys lived in style in a mansion on the river. Theirs was an over-the-top splendour he didn't envy. Although he'd met Huntley several times over the years, he'd never liked him, probably due to an abiding disgust with hypocrisy. Playing the part of devoted husband in public, it was common knowledge within the McCord family Huntley gave Carly a hard time. No one knew why she stayed with him. Apparently she was pretty much still in love with him. He was certainly impressive in his way, with his big, burly, dark hair, ice-blue eyes he had looks of a fading film star…

People were milling all over the house, drinking, standing, talking, dancing and generally having a good time. A very vivacious redhead—he swore she never touched a drink—had made a beeline for Jake as soon as he'd arrived. He didn't mind that as a matter of fact—she was attractive—but as the night wore on it became apparent the redhead had the vision of the two of them finishing up the evening in bed. It wasn't going to happen. He'd never said he was available.

At one point he sought refuge in what was presumably a study because the moment he opened the door, he saw a wall of books and trophies, dozens of them. A moment later he felt his insides contract as his eyes were led to where two people were locked into passionate lovemaking on the sofa.

He could hear the man's grunts of pleasure. See the rough way his hands moved. The woman was gorgeous, like something out of the Arabian Nights. She was dark-haired, great dark doe eyes. One beautiful breast with its dusky peak was totally exposed. The glimpse was blink-of-an-eye brief, yet he felt the heat of a flush spread like fire over his skin. Huntley was fondling the other breast, working the nipple, his harsh cries abruptly cutting off.

Carly's devoted Trevor. My God! He remembered the terrible sense of déjà vu. Huntley stood up staring, trying to adjust his clothing, unable to hide his arousal.

The woman buried her face in her trembling hands. Guilt? Shame? More likely she didn't want him to know her identity. "Disturbed you, did I?" He remembered his own voice, dripping acid. "Stupid of me not to knock." Hadn't the very same thing happened with Michelle? And Michelle had later claimed she wasn't even interested in the guy.

Huntley had actually given him a smile of undisguised insolence, the lust gleaming out of his eyes. "Welcome to the real world, my boy," he'd drawled, still fumbling with his clothing. "Don't look so shocked. I'm a man who always gets what he wants." He gestured to the young woman who was now sitting up on the sofa, pulling the thin strap that held up her bodice onto her shoulder, showing him only the naked gold satin of her back. "Do you blame me?"

How could he? He imagined his own hands on her. Felt instant self-disgust. He remembered he was badly shaken, alive with contempt. Now he was face-to-face with her.

The shock was so extreme he felt almost numb. This was the woman who had caused Carly so much suffering. Carly knew her husband had been having an affair, although, oddly, it wasn't this young woman who had figured in their spectacular divorce—Carly had used the family lawyers to secure a record settlement—it was a hard-faced blonde with the body of a stripper who was now the second Mrs. Huntley.

Jaw clenched, he forced himself to speak. "So you didn't go into hiding?"

"From you?" Angelica, too, was so traumatised she hardly knew what she was saying. Neither of them had made the slightest attempt to feign ignorance of the other. Both of them were instantly seized up by that shameful incident years before. Angelica's recollection of this man, however brief, was so acute, so agonising, she had to work hard to cope. Here was the tawny lion with a mane of deeply waving gold-streaked copper hair brushed back from a broad forehead. Could she ever mistake those distinctive amber eyes, or the condemnation in them? What inner trauma prompted that response?

This was the man who billowed in and out of her dreams. A man in full possession of himself and his world.

By a strange stroke of fate, Jake McCord. Her knees bumped together. "I wonder if I could ever convince you—" she began, turning away from the huge window.

The full glare of the sun was hitting her like a spotlight, finding no fault in her golden-olive skin. He cut her off swiftly. "Really, Miss De Campo, I don't want to know." She was still staggeringly beautiful, so lusciously ripe and alive, her skin so healthy and glowing it begged to be touched. How could a woman like that have allowed herself to be mixed up in such a murky demeaning affair? How could she have allowed herself to be mauled by a callous womaniser like Huntley?

She looked at him, upset, but very ready to defend herself. After all, she had done no wrong. She, like many another woman, had been the victim of a predatory man. "You're very judgmental, aren't you?" she said. "You really know nothing about what you saw years ago. I'm amazed you even remembered."

"You did, didn't you?" he countered, horrified by the harshness of his own tone, which in essence was an intertwining of past and present events. "I certainly didn't see you fending him off. God knows it couldn't have been that hard." His eyes swept her tall, svelte body. "Anyway, it no longer matters. Carly is re-making her life. Huntley's welcome to the ex-hooker he married. Didn't he want you after all?" He wondered why he asked, but was forced to confront the fact he really wanted to know. "Or didn't you want him?"

Her hair had come out of its too casual arrangement, dark masses of it atop her slender body. She put a hand to it. "You're taking this very hard, aren't you?"

"Hell, yes," he drawled. "Carly is part of my extended

family.'' And his mood was pervaded by a sense of deep disappointment.

''Have you ever tried to check out your theory with her?'' she questioned bluntly, not knowing any other way to put it.

''That you were having an affair with her ex-husband?'' he scoffed. ''Don't be ridiculous. God forbid I should have added to her worries.''

''You really should do something about your habit of jumping to conclusions, Mr. McCord,'' she suggested, seemingly unaware she was filling the air around them with her femininity and fragrance. ''One of these days, when you're prepared to listen, I'll tell you what it was all about.''

He laughed, ashamed of the swift desire he felt for her, though he had the wit to realise it was a matter outside his control. ''But, Miss De Campo, can't you see there's no way I'll listen. I regret the fact you've had to travel all the way out here, but I need to make a decision. In view of what we both know, and find embarrassing, I have to say you're not the woman I need to run our functions. I guess you're what most men would call a femme fatale. That's great up to a point, but I'm not paying for one to come out to Coori. Who knows how many guys might be prepared to make fools of themselves over you. There will be plenty around. Two polo teams, and you don't play by the rules. The womenfolk might hate you. I don't want to bump into you half-naked on a couch again either.''

''Why would you?'' she asked silkily. ''You couldn't handle it the first time. It seems to have burnt itself into your brain.''

''I'll get over it.'' He stood in front of her, shielding her from view, his face almost stern. ''You do understand my position?''

''Frankly, no.'' She tossed her exuberant mane, putting him in mind of a high-strung filly. ''We had a deal, Mr. McCord, and I'm going to hold you to it. I've put off other functions to come out here.''

''I'm quite prepared to compensate you for your trouble.''

"I'm sorry. I'm too full of pride. Right up to here!" She stepped forward and levelled a hand just beneath his arrogant nose. "I can't let you walk away from a commitment and I won't!"

"Really?" He raised a supercilious brow, hiding his unwilling admiration for her spirit. What would she be like if she were really angry? "Do you mind if we walk outside? We appear to be attracting quite a bit of attention." People were indeed looking their way, which might have a lot to do with her glorious appearance or the hostility of the body language.

"Well you will turn this into a crisis situation."

They walked out into the spiralling heat, the aromatic smell of baked earth and baked eucalyptus leaves blowing on the wind.

"Good grief, there's a kangaroo," she said, sounding as excited as a child about to make a spectacle of herself by running after it.

"You'll see plenty of them out here," he told her dryly, lulled by the lovely crooning quality of her voice.

"So I'm staying?" She turned to him hopefully, staring into his eyes. Playing him for all he was worth.

"It's hard to know what to do with you." His answer was therefore curt. At least it kept him from falling at her feet. If a latter day Cellini needed a model for the Roman goddess Venus, she was it. "I know in my bones, you're good old-fashioned Trouble."

"Would it help if I put on my half-moon reading glasses?" she asked with a kind of tart sweetness.

"You need glasses?" He felt a little shock. He didn't think she had a single flaw.

"Going on your masculine logic they might help," she answered with some of his own dryness.

"Well I've pretty much approved the mini-skirt," he told her coolly. "You don't feel self-conscious wearing it?"

"I'm not ashamed of my legs." She looked down at their

slender length, then at him. "Have you finished checking them out?"

Not half finished, he thought. "You're certainly very forthright, Miss De Campo." He glinted, inevitably reminded of the shy reticence of his stepmother and sister.

"What's good for the goose is good for the gander," she pronounced philosophically. "I insist now we hold to our agreement. From all accounts you need me."

"What do you mean?" For a moment hostility held sway. Had she heard some unkind comments about Stacy's lack of organisational skills?

"No need to bite my head off. I'm only saying, there's very little time to find my replacement even if I'd allow it. And I do have your initial cheque. Banked," she stressed.

"Is there any possibility you might accept it as compensation?" His expression hardened while he waited for her answer.

"None whatever. I've come, Mr. McCord, and I'm going to stay," she announced, exuding determination. "What's more, you'll find no fault with me. I intend to work as hard as I know how."

"Better yet you might think of a uniform." He glanced meaningfully at her well-endowed body, fighting down those unwelcome flares of excitement. "Keep it simple. Nothing revealing."

"You're very timid around women, aren't you?" She glanced at him sidelong. The man had sex appeal coming out of his ears. "Possibly you've had a bad experience?"

"One, but it was a long time ago. A femme fatale like you," he countered suavely, not allowing her to take a rise out of him. "You must understand your staying depends on true-blue behaviour, Miss De Campo."

"Angelica, please," she begged. "Angelica. Angie. I get both. But I'm not sure I know what true-blue behaviour is." She widened her beautiful eyes.

"It's not playing around," he explained. "Excuse the expression." To his consternation he found he was unable to look away from her luscious mouth.

Surprise flickered into her eyes. "You know you've got it all wrong." She gazed back with considerable appeal. "Huntley grabbed me," she told him simply. "I was such an idiot to go with him."

"Were you attracted to him?" It seemed both monstrous and bizarre.

"Lord, no!" She shuddered, making the clingy little top climb higher around her golden midriff. "Men like that I don't give the time of day."

"Really?" He'd heard something like this before. "Forgive me if I have to wonder why you were allowing him to maul you?"

"He was, wasn't he?" she agreed dismally. "All that grappling. I still remember the tumble on the couch. It wasn't my fault, I swear. But the way you were looking at me made me feel quite worthless. Odd to be innocent but found guilty." She pushed back tight little damp curls, marvelling at the heat. "He found an excuse to get me into the study. I was working with a colleague that night doing the catering."

"Did he send you a little note?"

"He spoke to me. He was the host. He was a big burly man who'd been tossing drinks down."

"I wouldn't call you little." Extravagantly beautiful, maybe.

"Mr. McCord, I've been insulted about my height all my life," she groaned.

"I don't believe that at all." She had to be fishing for compliments.

"Everyone called me Shorty at school. I know they were only joking but it hurt at the time."

"I suppose being so beautiful you needed the odd remark." The heat of the day wasn't bothering him, he was used to it, but he indicated they should move further under the shade of the trees. God help him if he actually touched her. She was dynamite. "Miss McCord, I don't feel in the least sorry for you," he told her briskly. "You're gorgeous. Have no doubts. One reason why I'm extremely anxious about taking you out to Coori."

"So when do we get started?" she asked with a surge of hope, absent-mindedly crumbling a dry eucalyptus leaf between her fingers, so she could enjoy the sharp nostalgic scent.

"The plane is over there." He pointed back through the trees to the light aircraft strip. It just so happened his was the only one there.

"My goodness! Unreal!" She gave a little gasp of admiration. "Your own private jet."

"It's not a jet, as you very well know. It's a Beech Baron."

"It's beautiful," she said, absolutely fascinated.

"Thank you." A shower of dry gum leaves suddenly fell from the trees, but he resisted the powerful impulse to brush them from her hair.

She shook her head, dislodging the burnished leaves herself. "Pardon my asking, but you don't have a lady friend to pull this off?"

"What off?" he retaliated sharply.

"Why, your functions, of course," she answered mildly. "I understand your stepmother and your sister, Gillian, are a little nervous about handling something so big?"

"Nice of Isobel to tell you." So they'd discussed it. Why not?

"She had to tell me," she answered with mild reasonableness, obviously a sunny-natured woman. "Not every woman wants to plunge into lots of catering activities. Fortunately for you, it so happens I love it."

"So I can point the finger at Isobel for telling you about my so-called lady friend?" He unleashed a certain toughness.

"Don't get cross," she coaxed. "You probably have no idea how ferocious you can look."

That rocked him. "I've hardly said a word." He imagined

a situation where he could simply pick her up and carry her off, caveman-style.

"You obviously don't mind getting personal?" She came a step further, strangely appealing in her tallness.

"I fail to see what's personal about that."

"Talking about the length of my skirt was. Your lady friend is a fellow rancher, I understand?"

He marvelled at her cheek, giving her a cool stare. "You're not getting paid to ask questions like that, Miss De Campo. As it happens, I'm a committed bachelor."

She didn't know if he was telling the truth or having her on. Not the time, really, to tell him he could very well be the man of her dreams. That would come later. Now she settled for, "You don't look like one." Indeed he looked like the hero of some big-budget adventure movie. The sort who kept a woman's eyes glued to the screen.

He didn't appear to be taking her seriously. In fact he moved off abruptly in the direction of his lovely plane, causing her to utilise some of what she thought of as her beanstalk height to catch up.

Equally abruptly, he turned back, smiling so tigerishly, he surprised her into slamming into him. Multiple little shocks like a charge of electricity rippled through her; a little sound suspiciously like excitement escaped her. The big cat's eyes swished over her.

"And you know them all?"

Angelica felt his condemnation like an actual burden. She didn't care how long it took, she'd convince him there'd been absolutely nothing between herself and Trevor Huntley, no matter what his eyes had deceived him into thinking. Things weren't always what they seemed yet he'd already brought in a verdict. It was awful to be accused of a crime like indecent exposure when one was perfectly innocent.

"So what about my luggage?" she prompted, although she'd just remembered it herself. Some measure of proof her customary aplomb had collapsed. "Surely you don't intend taking off without it?"

He laughed, a sexual sardonic sound. Something he was good at. "If all your clothes are as brief as what you're wearing," he observed, "I'm surprised you're not carrying it over your shoulder."

Good-natured as she was, she couldn't contain a flicker of temper. "Obviously you don't realise what's going on in women's fashions. I expect it comes with the landscape. You're a very long way from the big city."

"Which doesn't mean I don't get there part of the time to catch up." He hesitated a moment, his gleaming gaze speculative. "Any chance you've packed a few things a couple of inches longer?"

She responded sweetly though sparks were crackling between them. "To bring all this off successfully, and I so want to, Mr. McCord, perhaps I could arrange a showing of my wardrobe for you. You could tell me what you like and what you don't. The kind of thing a nice girl wears. We could talk about it."

His amber eyes sparkled with half malice, half amusement. "Which calls for time I don't have. You are the same woman I spoke to on the phone?"

"You have doubts?" She seemed to be gravitating towards him, drawn by his powerful magnetism.

"It is a concern," he mocked. "You don't seem like my initial choice."

"I'm me, I can vouch for it."

The handsomely defined mouth compressed. "In that case, you'd better come along. Your luggage, unless it's been stolen, should be beside the plane by now. I know the guy who drives the van."

"Let's hope he's not a cross-dresser," she joked.

"I beg your pardon." He paused to look down at her, eyes narrowed.

"I said—"

"I know what you said." Despite himself he had to laugh.

Whatever else the ravishingly wanton Miss De Campo might prove to be—and he just knew she was going to be an extravagant handful—she wouldn't be dull. That's what he had liked about her in the first place.

CHAPTER THREE

FROM the air, Coori homestead, surrounded by its satellite buildings, resembled a settlement constructed on the site of an oasis. The vast areas around it, thousands upon thousands of square miles, in comparison, was practically the far side of planet Mercury. The burning, mirage-stalked earth was coloured a brilliant red, scattered densely with golden bushes like great mounds. Angelica guessed before McCord told her it was spinifex. Spinifex and sand. Out here the two went together.

"The cattle will eat it if nothing else is available," he told her casually, secretly pleased she'd been such a good passenger. She was fearless—they'd hit a few thermals—she showed great interest in her latest adventure, and she asked intelligent questions. "But spinifex has little food value for the stock. The seeds on the other hand we use to fatten horses to prime condition."

"From here it looks rather like wheat," she observed, fascinated by the spectacle, the sheer size and emptiness of a giant primitive landscape that was crisscrossed by maze after maze of water channels—swamps, lagoons, billabongs, desert streams—that appeared to be running near dry.

He nodded. "Especially at this time of year. The interior of the bushes, strangely enough, is quite cool. For that reason the lizards make their home there, but the wax content is so high the bushes can burn fiercely. When they do, they send up great clouds of black smoke for days."

"It doesn't look like you've had any rain," she said quietly, thinking drought must be really terrible to the man on the land.

His laugh was ironic. "Not for a year. Not a drop during

winter-spring. Not a single shower, but we've seen great displays of storm-clouds like a Wagnerian set that got wheeled away. We're hoping the Wet season up north will be a good one. But not too good. We can do without the floods. Just enough to flush out every water channel. When the eastern river system comes down in flood, the waterbirds fly in in their millions. The Channel Country is a major breeding ground for nomadic waterbirds. Great colonies of Ibis nest in our lignum swamps. They do us a big favour by feasting on the destructive flocks of grasshoppers that strip the grass and herbage for the stock. Then there are all sorts of ducks in their countless thousands—herons, shags, spoonbills, waterhens, egrets.''

''So where do they come from?'' she asked, turning to admire his handsome profile. He was a marvellous-looking man.

''Good question. No one seems to know. It's one of those great mysteries of the Outback. One day there's not a sign of them, but then a sudden storm, the billabongs fill and they're there literally overnight. Most other birds take days to arrive, when they sense water. Pelicans—I love the pelicans. I used to try to find their nests as a boy—turn up in favoured years to breed in our more remote swamps. Those are just the waterbirds. What will dazzle you here is the great flights of budgerigar, a phenomenon of the Outback, like the crimson chats and the finches. The hawks and the falcons prey on them. The largest bird is the wedge-tailed eagle. You'll identity it easily in flight from the wingspan. At least seven foot. The wingtips curve up. Wedge-tails can take a fair-size kangaroo.''

''Goodness.'' She tried to visualise it. ''Swooping on a medium-size kangaroo must take some doing?''

''They don't have a problem. There are plenty of predators around.'' He shrugged. ''The huge flocks of white birds you'll see are the corellas. They cover the coolabahs so densely you can scarcely see a leaf. Or a branch. And the noise when they take off is deafening. All our beautiful parrots prefer the scrub. Not that you'll have much time for sight-seeing, Miss De Campo. You're here to work.''

"I'll get up very early," she murmured. "What a truly extraordinary place you live in." It had to have moulded him, made him special. "You must feel like a desert chieftain?"

He glanced at her with those amazing exotic eyes. Everything about him said, "Don't go trying to fascinate me." What a challenge! He confirmed it by saying, "Don't go getting any romantic notions. I'm a hardworking cattleman. I haven't the energy to ravish females."

"I guess desert chieftains don't have to be mad rapists," she joked.

"Have you been raped?" he asked very seriously indeed, giving her a direct stare. Huntley, brute that he was, was probably capable of it. That, he couldn't bear.

"No such terrible thing has happened to me, the Lord be praised." She shuddered. "No woman knows for certain if she's going to be in the wrong place at the wrong time. It's woman's universal fear. I have a guardian angel I pray to to look after me. A father who adores me. A brother who thinks a lot of me. He's built like a commando and he has a black belt."

"Whereas all you've got is a cupboard full of basketball trophies."

"I'm sorry I told you that," she said.

"You also told me you were frequently asked, 'How's the weather up there?' "

"My favourite was how did I cope with altitude sickness. People are cruel. The plainer they are, the crueller they get."

"Whereas you're a most beautiful woman."

"Am I?" she asked with a small degree of surprise. She'd had plenty of compliments in her time but she hadn't been expecting too many from him. Not after that flinty-eyed reception.

"Miss De Campo, I have no intention of going soft on you," he assured her, as though he found her mind easy to read. "I hope you believe it, though I'm sure your successes have been legion. I'll be watching your every move. You may have won the battle but not the war."

"Why should there be war between us? A war would get us nowhere. I'm looking for your co-operation."

"And you'll get it providing you don't take it into your head to send the senses of the male population reeling."

"As though I'd be capable of such a thing," she answered breezily. "Are we coming in to land?"

"We are," he confirmed crisply, thinking he was coming off second best with this woman. "So you can tighten your seat belt."

"Aye, aye, Captain!" She laughed as excitement set in. "Or is it 'Roger?' I have to catch up on the terminology. Anyway, I can't wait." She looked down, trying to gather in her kaleidoscope of thoughts and impressions. "Obviously it's all paid off, being a desert chieftain," she enthused. "The homestead looks huge!" And the setting was fantastic! "Who would ever have thought of building a mansion in the middle of the Never-Never?"

"We are a way out of town," he agreed dryly. "Do you think you can possibly sit quietly?"

"Just watch me." She gave him a cheerful smile, proceeding to sit as solidly as an Easter Island statue. Honey caught more flies than vinegar. Hadn't her mother told her?

They were greeted by a station hand the moment they arrived. When the young man was introduced to Angelica he muttered a, "Pleased to meet you," without lifting his head. Indeed he seemed dead-set on digging the toe of his riding boot into the baked earth.

"Shy," Angelica commented kindly when she and McCord had disposed themselves in the waiting Jeep.

"Why not?" McCord gave her a sidelong glance. "Noah was brought up in the bush. He's never seen a woman like you in his life."

"Aw shucks!" she pretended to simper. "You'll be telling me you had me pegged for a high-class callgirl in two ticks."

"You have to admit we started badly."

"You being so judgmental. The fact of the matter is you owe me an apology." She lifted her chin as she spoke. It had a shallow dimple he really loved. Not that he was about to tell her that.

"I'll apologise if I have to when I know the true story," he assured her. "Huntley had several girlfriends and a mistress at the time. Carly knew for a fact at least one was a very glamorous brunette. That doesn't exactly clear you."

"It doesn't condemn me, either," she said tartly. "I don't want to insult you but you sound a real prude."

"Your opinion, Miss De Campo, doesn't concern me at all. I know what I saw in that study. People were milling about. You could have screamed. You could have appealed to me for help. Had you needed it. I would have enjoyed knocking dear Trevor flat."

"I regret to say I was too ashamed and mortified," Angelica confessed, appalled to hear her excuse sound so weak. "Seconds elapsed from the moment he got me into that study to when he all but threw me on the sofa."

He made no attempt to hide a snort of derision. "You're not exactly a featherweight. Come to think of it, my recollection of you is a lot of woman."

"A lot?" she burst out wrathfully. "Don't be ridiculous. I was a comfortable size twelve."

"Are you sure?" He did his best to look sceptical. "Not that I know much about women's dress sizes, but being in the cattle business I'm a good judge of weight. I'd say you were a good stone heavier then."

"Well, perhaps," she conceded, pulling a face. How did he know so much when he'd only see her for such a short time? "These days I go to the gym. And I watch my diet. I've actually worked out quite a care program. Especially now I'm on the TV. I know I'm a big girl."

"Big is beautiful," he returned, a sardonic gleam in his amber gold-speckled eyes. "There's hardly a thing to choose between you and a supermodel."

When they stepped into the splendid entrance hall of Coori

homestead a cute young woman around five-two, with fair hair and sky-blue eyes, dressed in cotton jeans and a T-shirt, rushed down the central staircase to greet them. "Oh, you're here! That's lovely!" she cried enthusiastically, directly addressing Angelica and waggling her fingers at her half brother as though he'd pulled off a great coup. "Isobel didn't exaggerate. You're beautiful!"

It sure beat her half brother's reception, Angelica thought, immediately warming to Gillian. This girl fitted Isobel's description. Gillian was just possibly half a foot, maybe more, shorter, but what the heck! Angelica was comforted by such a welcome. "How nice of you to say so." She held out her hand, returning the beaming smile.

McCord's young half sister was a mixture of shyness and appealing vulnerability. She bore no resemblance whatsoever to her half brother. "You're Gillian, of course."

"Gilly, please." Gillian took the hand extended to her, staring up at Angelica with the kind of heroine worship one usually saw reserved for school captain. "Mum will be here in a moment," she explained. "This is the second time she's changed her dress. Isobel told us you've got great style."

"You should have seen some of my fashion disasters," Angelica confided, refusing to look in McCord's direction, in case he was still critically examining her denim mini.

"I'm sure you'd look wonderful in anything," Gillian said so sincerely Angelica wanted to hug her.

"Listen, why don't we let Miss De Campo settle in," McCord suggested, his tone an unexpected combination of gentleness and wry impatience.

Gillian blushed. "Sorry, Jake."

"No worries, Gilly." He lightly touched her shoulder. "Has anything happened while I've been gone? Any messages?"

"Oh." Gilly made an apologetic little sound. "I nearly forgot. The vet can make it this afternoon, after all. He'll be here around three-thirty. He's cadged a ride with Brodie.

Brodie brings the mail and supplies,'' she explained to Angelica in an aside.

"A bit of good news. Anything else?'' McCord prompted patiently. Angelica got the feeling he did that often.

"Dinah rang.'' Gillian started to gnaw at one of her fingernails. "She's flying over Friday afternoon. She thought she might stay the weekend. Invited herself really.'' She slumped as though the high-handed Dinah was already there. "She says she can't wait to meet Angelica.''

"And Dinah is?'' Angelica neatly questioned, more than halfway to knowing she was one of McCord's girlfriends. No revelation a man like that would have a huge following and she couldn't now overlook herself.

"Friend of the family,'' he clipped off, obviously not wanting to be pushed into any discussion. "Now I've a few things to do before I show you around, Angelica.'' He gave her a smile of such lazy sensuality Angelica almost swooned. "Meanwhile, Gilly can help you settle in. Your luggage will be at your door. The day will be over before I get out there but I'm leaving you in good hands.''

"Thanks, Jake!'' Gillian smiled happily.

"See you in about an hour.'' He gave Angelica another one of those looks that sizzled.

She had a mad desire to call after him, "Have fun now,'' but wisely thought better of it. McCord was obviously a man to be reckoned with. He probably spent all his days giving orders and being obeyed. It was too bad about this Dinah. Then again, she reminded herself, he wasn't engaged. Not surprising when he had described himself as a committed bachelor, but she had the feeling that was a big hint for her. Not exactly a propitious beginning for both of them, but she refused to allow it to dampen her buoyant spirits. She had only set foot on Coori and already she was in love with its wild beauty, its history and romance. All right! The master of Coori wasn't too bad, either.

The mistress of that great station—one of the shyest people Angel had met, even more startling considering the power and influence of the family—gazed at Angelica a minute or two, then gave her an unreserved welcome that was as warm and informal as that of her daughter's.

"Oh, I'm so glad it's you," she confided sometime later, as they relaxed over iced tea. "Isobel is a dear woman— she's been very kind to me—but she's so confident in every way she makes me feel a desperate failure. You and I are going to get on well."

That shook Angelica a little. She took the frosted mint-scented glass from her mouth. "You think I'm going to make lots of mistakes?"

"Oh, no, dear, I'm sure you won't." Stacy was astonished at Angelica's quite logical interpretation. "You have that un-mistakable touch of class, and laughter in your eyes. An ease of manner I find very soothing. I know you won't make me feel nervous. Beautiful women have made me nervous all my life."

"Maybe you haven't noticed I'm oversize." Angelica smiled.

"That's the surprising thing," Stacy said artlessly. "It looks just right on you. I, on the other hand, have always struggled to attain any sort of stature." She looked vaguely around the lovely sitting room furnished with a mixture of contemporary and antique pieces. "I was never right as mis-tress of Coori station, for instance. I'm sure you've already heard that from Isobel. Why Clive picked on humble little me remains a puzzle in the McCord family. He should have kept looking. Jake is very tolerant of my lack of organisa-tional skills. He's been my champion since he was a little boy. Not that it did him any good. Clive couldn't tolerate the way Jake stood up to him. I think he found it threatening, even allowing for the hard man that he was. Jake can be tough when he has to be, but he has heart. My late husband was a heartless perfectionist."

Angelica had heard that, as well, but still felt shocked. "That must have been hard to live up to?"

"Oh, it runs in the family," Stacy sighed. "Thank the Lord, Jake is different. His father was from the school of biting sarcasm. It was easy to make him explode. No matter how much I tried to please him, I couldn't. The irony is, it was my only ambition."

Angelica shook her head in sympathy, nevertheless surprised by Stacy's disclosures so early in their acquaintance. She tinked the rim of her crystal glass against her white teeth. What a life it must have been, to be constantly belittled. She believed her own mother, wife, earthmother, restauranteur, superstar, would have put Clive McCord right. Men seemed to pick their mark. On the face of it Stacy McCord seemed like a natural-born victim. There wasn't going to be any small talk, either. Stacy had major traumas to unload with seemingly not a minute to lose.

"Of course in my youthful ignorance I thought loving him was enough," Stacy continued in that soft reminiscent voice. It wasn't often she found herself with a captive audience, consequently she found it difficult not to keep going. "Clive was everything I dreamed about. I thought I was in for a life of married bliss, a home of my own where I could be in charge for a change. And my parents were over the moon with such a splendid match. The McCords are an old pioneering family."

"And rich?" That upped anyone's eligibility, Angel thought.

"There's always something about money," Stacy agreed. "It made my mother so happy. She was proud of me for once. But the money didn't mean anything to me. I loved him. He was such a striking-looking man and I was little more than a silly schoolgirl. I didn't have a glimmer of an idea he'd bought me like he'd buy a pedigreed little heifer. I was young and pretty, if you can believe it. I was soft, and by the way I mean soft in the head, as well. I had no instinct for trouble. I didn't even notice Clive wasn't a bit of fun."

By this time Angelica herself didn't know whether to laugh or cry. "I doubt many people have it all together at eighteen,'' she consoled. I mean, did she? The answer was a resounding no. ''It takes time to understand human emotions and passions. If we ever do. Anyway there's nothing like getting married to bring out the best and worst in people.''

Stacy, to her credit, gave vent to a surprisingly hearty laugh. ''Why is it I think I've known you forever?''

''It happens like that.'' Angelica smiled.

''But I am talking too much.'' Stacy suddenly flushed, blotching her apple-blossom skin.

''I really appreciate the fact you trust me,'' Angelica told her with sincerity. The fact of the matter was she often received unsolicited confidences the moment people laid eyes on her. She supposed she must look kind, or they thought they'd never see her again. She'd even received off-the-cuff marriage proposals.

''I used to think if the portrait of Roxanne came down, Clive would start to forget.'' Stacy pushed at her wispy fringe, a mannerism Angelica had remarked. ''But he never did. He was absolutely faithful to her to the end. I suspect when he was dying alone out there in the desert he cried out her name. Maybe they're together again at last.''

''Maybe they are,'' Angelica said, with a kind of fascinated sadness. If she were a romance writer instead of a caterer she could have turned the whole thing into a blockbuster. ''I believe in an afterlife, but you have to let go, Stacy.''

Stacy nodded. Nodded again with great vehemence. ''Oh, it's so good to talk. Very few would be interested.''

''You're still young.'' Angelica intuited Stacy had been thinking along these lines. ''There's no reason why you can't re-marry. Happily this time. Life goes by so fast you have to grab it on the wing.''

''Oh, God!'' Stacy exclaimed almost despairingly. ''That's all very well for you. You're young and so vibrant. I don't believe I ever was. I was Little Miss Helpless. Only child syndrome. Older parents. Anyway, who'd have me?''

''A lot,'' Angelica answered dryly.

"Aha, the money." Stacy saw the irony.

"Don't put yourself down. You're a pretty woman."

"Am I?" Stacy sounded pleased and even took a very human little peek into a well-positioned gilded mirror. "But how could I meet anyone out here?"

"Dive right in," Angelica advised. "We have all these wonderful Christmas functions coming up. I absolutely love Christmas. We must have a great big tree. I know you've got one."

"No we haven't got one," Stacy announced surprisingly. "Clive only died three years ago. He didn't want any Christmas trees."

"Why didn't you get one yourself? Even afterwards?" Angelica was so amazed, her voice cracked.

"I think I expected Clive might come back to haunt me. Anyway if I put up a big Christmas tree you can count on its falling over."

"It won't fall over on me," Angelica said. "Have we agreed on a Christmas tree? I know exactly where it should go. The bigger the better."

"We've no pines here, dear, only desert oaks." Stacy smiled.

"We'll find something," Angelica said. "But getting back to our functions, you know who's coming. Surely there's an eligible man or two? There must be, I can see you smiling."

"Really just a friend." Stacy's voice softened. A dead give-away. "He's a lovely man, but I can't think he'd be all that interested in me. There are others."

"Look on the positive side," Angelica advised. "You can have what you want if you go after it. I've found it really doesn't pay to be tentative and hold back. Why don't we try to sort things out this week? I'm going to have to press you into service, if that's okay? No need to worry. You're going to enjoy it. Have fun. Offering hospitality to friends should be fun. You don't have to perform miracles. Gillian has to do her bit, too. Is there a guy in her life?"

Stacy glanced over her shoulder as though Gillian was

about to return. "Gilly's got a crush on one of our jackeroos," she confided.

Angelica's jaw dropped. She thought jackeroos were supposed to keep their distance. "Really?"

"He's a fine young man, but he's English."

Angelica, disconcerted, just stopped herself from snorting. "Is that a problem?" She stared at Stacy, wondering if Stacy had been hoping for a local.

"It is in this way…" Stacy started to clarify. "Charlie could go back home at any time. He's here for the adventure. He read all about the Outback as a boy and fancied himself living the frontier life. They must have made it sound very glamorous. Anyway he loves it but his family will want him back home. Who could blame them? He's the Honourable Charles Middleton by the way."

Angelica was fascinated. "That sounds safe enough. You mean Gillian has a member of the English aristocracy in her pocket?"

"Well, it hasn't gone far, but they seem very fond of each other. Charlie is such a nice young man. Jake likes him, too, which makes things so much easier. That's where she's nipped out to."

"To see Charlie?" Angelica asked, further intrigued.

"They don't go a day without seeing each other." Stacy brushed at her fringe, torn between feeling happy for her daughter and worry. "I pray and pray she won't get hurt. I mean, she's a real softie like me."

"And the Honourable Charlie isn't your normal, average guy." Angelica nodded in understanding. "This must be an entirely new way of life for him?"

"You'd think he was born to it." Stacy smiled fondly. "Though he's had his learning curve. He finished up in hospital last year with a back injury. We were all so worried, but he made an excellent recovery. Jake keeps in contact with his family and of course Charlie does, too, but his father likes Jake to tell him how his son is getting along. I suppose you could call him much more than the normal jackeroo. He often comes up to the house for dinner. He hero worships Jake. He thinks he's marvellous even when Jake has had to tear strips off him for being too reckless. But those were the early days.''

"I'm looking forward to meeting Charlie.'' Angelica had to laugh.

Please don't take him off Gilly, Stacy thought. Most men wouldn't be able to tear their eyes away from Angelica. But she seemed such a nice girl. Generous and kind.

They were still chatting when Jake returned. He heard their laughter as he made his way to his stepmother's sitting room. Miss De Campo certainly knew how to charm people, he thought. Every time Dinah came over there was no hint of laughter from Stacy or Gilly.

Both women looked up as he entered the cool, charming room. "How's it going?''

"We haven't stopped talking from the moment we sat down,'' Stacy told him, pink-cheeked and happy. "In fact I haven't enjoyed myself so much in ages.''

"That's good.'' Miss De Campo was either very kind or very clever. Maybe both. He glanced at her. She had changed her eye-catching mini for an equally hot little number; a cool white cotton knit top over pink cotton jeans that sat as sweetly on her hips as the oval-dipping top clung to her breasts. She had a major talent for wearing clothes. It was no problem to imagine her naked, either. "If we're going to look around, we'd better get started,'' he said, sounding crisp.

"Fine!'' Instantly, Angelica jumped to her feet. "I can't wait to see around. My bedroom is simply beautiful. Very grand.''

"I decided on it, dear.'' Stacy looked pleased.

"A four-poster is a real treat for me.'' Angelica said. "I'm really going to enjoy myself going to bed.''

You'd make me pretty damned happy, as well, Jake thought, not insured against dangerous thoughts.

They made a tour of the house, moving from room to room

of the mansion. They started with the reception rooms but Jake took little time in the beautiful Yellow Drawing Room that housed the portrait of his mother, and Angelica sensed some inner emotional struggle. They spent more time over the very fine library with its collection of rare books, and now they stood inside Clive McCord's memento- and trophy-filled study, a room Jake told her he didn't use.

Eyes dark and brilliant, Angelica looked up at the portrait of Clive McCord that dominated the generously sized room. "I must be a fanciful person but I feel the people who lived in this house all around us," she said quietly. "There's been happiness here, hope, love and sorrow."

"Certainly my father waged his own personal war against fate," Jake said without bitterness, looking into his father's painted piercingly blue eyes. He looked wonderfully handsome, arrogant, with the promise of a glorious life ahead of him. This had been painted as a companion piece to the portrait of his mother in the Yellow Drawing Room.

"It was wrong of him to make his family suffer," Angelica said gently, "but the joy must have gone out of him the day your mother was killed." She turned to look into Jake's handsome face. It wore a sombre expression, as though he remembered constant duels in this very room.

"I hate to admit it." He shrugged. "I'm a grown man, but he hurt us all. He never treated me like a son. More like a usurper whose only aim was to steal his throne from him. Contradictory really because my father always said life was meaningless."

"I expect he meant without your mother. It was very hard on Stacy."

"She told you?" And if she did, who did Stacy really have to talk to?

"Why not? Stacy accepts me as the person I am."

"Whereas I've dipped into your past?" he murmured, thinking how that had complicated things.

"Is it you don't trust me or you don't trust anyone?" she asked directly.

Something flashed in his eyes. "Maybe I'm more like my father than I care to acknowledge."

"Is that a fear?" Both her voice and her expression was very soft, near tender.

It affected him so much he wanted to grab her. Pull her into his arms. Rain kisses down on the luscious mouth. Instead he said coolly, "Is this a psychoanalysis session?"

"I think life would be unendurable if we couldn't talk to someone," she countered, realising there was a lot of stress in him.

"I don't know you..." He only had to lower his head.

"Strangely, I don't feel like that." The atmosphere was so intimate she found herself near whispering. "I think you fall into the category of people I've known in another life."

"How fanciful...Angel." Now why had he called her that?

On his lips it sounded heavenly. "Millions of people believe in reincarnation," she said, her blood racing. "I still say I met you somewhere along the way."

"And did you love me or hate me?" he asked, some note in his voice sending shock waves along her nerves.

"I don't know," she admitted, her voice so breathy it touched his cheek. "But I know you. I can't explain it." She looked back at the portrait of Clive McCord. "That's a very powerful painting. Clearly you don't have your father's colouring, but you do have a look of him."

"So tell me, is it the arrogance?"

"You might have a touch of it but I should think it was the arrogance of achievement. I think you're going to be a winner in life's battles, Jake McCord."

He tried to clear the huskiness from his throat. "Who taught you how to heal?" he asked.

She looked at him in surprise. "I'm not aware I have that talent."

His amber gaze was brilliant and unblinking. "I swear you've been using it on me since the moment you stepped off the plane."

"Maybe I'm looking for the man behind the tough fa-
çade." A beautiful smile moved over her face. "My poppa
is a little bit like you. Very much the dominant male in the
old tradition but he has a sweet centre. My mother soon
found it."

He was close enough to touch her. To run his fingers down
her cheek, brush back the glossy dark tumble of hair. He did
none of those things. Instead he asked, "Are you saying you
could find mine? Always supposing I have one."

"You must!" She shrugged an elegant satiny shoulder.
"Stacy and Gilly love you."

"So basically I'm a good guy," he said with wry humour.

"That's about the size of it." She glanced up at him,
looked away quickly before he saw invitation in her eyes.
For reasons she couldn't entirely fathom she found this complex man utterly irresistible. This man who for his own reasons had decided to condemn her. But such was the power
of attraction, irrational in its way. She made a silent vow to
find the real man beneath. Jake McCord was one enigma she
intended to solve.

CHAPTER FOUR

ONCE in a blue moon did you see showcase country kitchens like this, Angelica thought, pausing in the open doorway to admire the extraordinarily inviting king-size room. It was a delightful mix of old and new with homestead charm allied to the finest modern appliances money could buy. Such a highly functional kitchen with plenty of work spaces would make her job so much easier. In fact it would have fitted seamlessly into her parents' flagship Italian restaurant.

Her trained eye moved with approval over marble bench tops, lots of gleaming timber—cupboards, a polished hardwood floor—a timber hanging rail displaying copper utensils above a huge central work station. Along the back wall, a restaurant-size stainless-steel oven, stainless-steel refrigerators with matching freezers side by side. There was even a small informal dining area, circular table and four cottage chairs by the window where deflected sunlight streamed in. On the centre of the table stood a bright ceramic bowl full of lemons. A must in any cook's kitchen.

The housekeeper—for a godsend, they had met and taken to one another on sight—preferred to be known only as "Clary." The name suited her, Angel thought, uncertain whether Clary by chance stood for Clara, Clarice or even Clarabelle. No one had enlightened her if they even knew.

Clary would have been well into her sixties conforming to the traditional idea of "cook," stout of figure with an air of great energy, shrewd, genial eyes and a fine head of thick pepper-and-salt curls. Given the size of the homestead and the family and the stacks of visitors to the station to feed Angel could well see she would always be on the go. In a year or two, maybe less, Clary would surely want to retire

and have some time to herself. Apparently she had been running the household since it was discovered the second Mrs.
McCord had little aptitude for the job. Coming up twenty
years? In that time Clary had created her own super-
functional, super-efficient kitchen environment over which
she reigned supreme.

As Angelica stood admiring a world-renowned double
cooker, Clary emerged from an adjacent doorway to the rear.
"Hello there, Clary," Angelica called, her admiring voice
not lost on the housekeeper. "I hope I'm not disturbing you.
I was just looking at your marvellous kitchen."

"You can disturb me all you like, love," Clary said comfortably, waving a hand to welcome Angelica in. "I take that
as a real compliment coming from you. I see copies of
Cosima, you know. I really like the way you write. It's infectious. And I like your recipes with all the little surprises.
You make food preparation fun."

"Which, of course, it is if you love food and all the wonderful produce of the earth. I must say you've a splendid
working environment here," Angelica commented, running
a hand over a bench top. "Great for serious cooking. It will
make the job of catering so much easier."

"That it will," Clary agreed, picking up a dish cloth to
wipe away a non-existent spot. "Would you like to look at
the pantry, love. It's well stocked but you'll be wanting lots
more. You do need a hand?"

"You bet I do, Clary. I'm counting on it."

"I'm in." Clary injected pleasure and enthusiasm into it.
"Isobel appreciates my help, too. We want to do Coori
proud. You won't get Stacy, God love her, on the team
though," she added wryly. "She's not domesticated, I'm
afraid, but Isobel would have told you that. In the early days
I used to try to show her something but she always disappeared. It used to make the master simmer, I can tell you,
but it seemed to make no impression on Stacy. She didn't
always pick up on his moods. You know and I know that to
feed people successfully, come up with menus, et cetera, you

have to love food. Like it at least. Stacy and young Gilly only eat to survive. They have little interest in what I put before them.''

Angelica, an inspired cook, who thought every woman should know her way around a kitchen, was seized by empathy. ''Gosh, that can't make you happy?''

''Especially when you're asked for toast and a boiled egg. I've been here a long time.'' Clary shrugged. ''The master, Mr. Clive, demanded the best. He grew up with his own father and mother priding themselves on keeping a good table. If one tiny thing was omitted, it was a crime as far as he was concerned. Lord could he be fierce! I dunno that I've met a worse man to this day. When I first came here I was tempted to kill him with one of my favourite kitchen knives.''

''You never considered doing a runner instead?'' Angelica laughed.

''No, love. I was down on me luck. I stuck it out. He wasn't miserable with money. I was well paid and I came to love Jake. I had no kids and loving him was the easiest thing imaginable. He was a great little guy, so brave and spirited with his father I used to get anxious for him, but he just kept getting better and better. Now he's the boss, the Lord be praised. To work for him is a pleasure. Jake truly appreciates a good meal. Sometimes I can't fill him. He works too hard. That's what worries me. He runs Coori and the out-stations and that's not his only role. He does the lot around here. When his father was alive Jake had to work until he dropped. But he hung in because Coori is his heritage.''

''A marvellous heritage,'' Angelica said fervently, pleasantly stunned the household with the exception of McCord were only too ready to confide in her.

''The best!'' Clary agreed. ''This is the pantry, love,'' she announced, waving her hand around a mini-supermarket. ''Everyday household. There are store rooms, refrigerator rooms elsewhere in the compound. We supply our own beef, lamb, pork, poultry, game. I make a beautiful red Thai kangaroo curry with coconut rice. I pride myself on keeping up with the latest trends as well as the old favourites. Of course kangaroo isn't everyone's cup of tea. A bit gamey for some, but I do some lovely cured char-grilled topside steaks, as well.''

''They'll probably go well with the barbecue,'' Angelica said. ''I have to admit I'm a bit emotional about Skippy, kangaroos being the national emblem and all. At the same time I realise we have a superb renewable resource. We'd be foolish to forget that.''

''God knows there are enough of them,'' Clary remarked. ''The annual cull is carried out under the supervision of National Parks and Wildlife. Some years when water is plentiful they're a real menace.''

''So I understand. Sometime tomorrow, Clary, when you have a minute, I'd like to sit down with you and plan out what we're going to do. We're not getting into complex food, or anything that is time-consuming. It's all about taste and using the freshest, best possible ingredients as well as providing warm hospitality. Polo day's first up. Lunch, afternoon tea. Neither will present a problem. It'll take more time working out supper for the ball.''

''Staff barbecue, no worries, either,'' Clary said. ''We're all used to them. I get lots of help from the station wives and the older kids home from boarding school. Everyone pitches in. They love it.''

''Great! Then there's the Christmas party. We'll go to town on that. And I'm so looking forward to decorating the house. Such a marvellous house! So very grand. I can feel the history. Stacy tells me you haven't had a Christmas tree since she's been here.''

Clary looked at her with a sad expression. ''The first Mrs. McCord, Jake's mother was killed just before Christmas. You didn't know that, love?''

''No.'' Angelica shook her dark head, instantly upset she might have put her foot in it.

''The master never came to terms with that.''

''I would think not. No birthday parties, either?''

"Gracious, did Jake tell you that?" Clary looked at her with admiration.

"Only in passing, as a joke."

"It was no joke," Clary said. "I know it sounds disloyal, but the master was no bundle of laughs."

"Well, Jake is McCord now. The Christmas tree will be a start. I'll be speaking to him tonight about it. We need a ceiling on the budget."

"It won't be tight, love," Clary assured her as Angelica began to walk up and down the aisles that divided the huge pantry with Clary trailing her.

"Clary this is fantastic!"

"We're so isolated, love, we can't have provisions flown in all the time. I need to make the ordering cost-effective. I handle all that side of it and I have my small staff. My girls are all part aboriginal. They're more like domestic apprentices. Leah, in particular, is very good. I rely on her a lot and don't have to keep checking all the time. She has a little daughter, Kylee. Kylee's nearly four. She's as cute as they come. Leah was treated badly by the white man who fathered her child. As soon as she fell pregnant he abandoned her. She had no money and nowhere to go. The child was born on one of the McCord out-stations. Jake gave her a job."

"That was good of him."

"He's a very responsible man. Practically a saint," Clary said earnestly. "He also put out the word. The father had to move on. He couldn't land another stockman's job in this part of the world again."

"How old is Leah?" Angelica asked, looking through a variety of staple tinned products.

"Early twenties, I reckon. She doesn't really know. She's had a hard life has our little Leah. She was removed from abusive parents."

"The abuse continued," Angelica said briefly, and shook her head.

"There's a pattern," Clary agreed sadly. "Clever little thing, too. I'd like you to meet her."

"I'll look forward to it." Angelica said, her voice resonating warmly. "Little Kylee, too. What's Christmas without children? She's going to love the Christmas tree. Now what's on the menu for tonight?"

"You mean, dinner?" For a minute Clary looked the happiest woman in the world.

"I do, too." Angelica gave her a smile that made Clary smile, too.

"You're going to put me on my mettle, aren't you?"

"I fancy you'll like that, Clary," Angelica teased.

The rest of the day melted into a flurry of activity for Angelica. With Clary well and truly onside, the task ahead of her seemed less formidable. Jake had set aside a station vehicle, a four-wheel drive, for her and she simply took off, driving around the compound and the plains beyond, grateful for the cream akubra Gillian had lent her and her own excellent sunglasses to ward off the worst of the shimmering heat.

Following Stacy's somewhat hazy instructions she found the polo fields, and gave a lot of thought to where she would set up the marquees. It had emerged in the course of conversation Jake was a marvellous player, physically and mentally tough, with wonderful co-ordination and balance. He was also captain of one of the teams contesting the Marsdon Polo Cup. She had looked the event up. She'd also read up about the game of polo knowing it was *the* game out here. Apparently the rules were quite complex so she was far from perfect on them. She'd just have to score a few points as a spectator, looking as glamorous as she possibly could. She had a great outfit anyway. She was looking forward to seeing Jake all dressed up in his polo gear, the numbered shirt, the white breeches, long boots and helmet. No wonder some women developed a mad passion for polo players.

When she saw the Great Hall she stood for a long time, arms folded, visualising what she wanted to do with the decoration. She stared up at the ceiling. Wouldn't it be great painted, perhaps a beautiful deep blue? Maybe studded with the moon and stars? Or better yet in keeping with the polo theme, floating umbrellas amid the clouds, like the ones spectators gathered under at a swank Sydney polo club she had been taken to as a visitor. She wondered what McCord would say to that idea. When she'd spoken to him on the phone that first night he'd managed to convey to her she could have her heart's desire. That was before they had meet face to face and the whole embarrassing Huntley affair with its long lingering sense of shame had rocked her respectable status and established suspicious beginnings.

Late afternoon saw her standing on the broad verandah of the upper storey, watching heat lightning flash up against an incredible sunset of blazing reds, pinks and golds. It speared forks of purple, livid green, indigo and yellow into the billowing clouds. Now nothing moved. Fifteen minutes before, the sky was a moving spectacle of birds of all colours, brilliant parrots, wave upon wave of emerald bolts of silk, the budgerigar, pink and grey galahs, the pure white sulphur-yellow-crested cockatoos, all trying to get home before the storm. A storm that never eventuated though she couldn't imagine it wasn't coming.

She was so absorbed in looking at the blazing, bruised, sky she didn't notice Jake McCord moving down the verandah towards her until he was almost upon her.

"Nothing will come of it, if that's what you're wondering," he said, tilting the akubra he wore at a rakish swagger. So catlike was his tread, she actually jumped, one hand to her heart.

"You startled me," she said unsteadily. And that wasn't the main problem. He deeply stirred and disturbed her. Once more she hoped he couldn't see her reactions to him in her face and misinterpret them as some sort of a come-on.

"I'm sorry. Shall I go back and start again?" The golden-amber eyes danced over her, causing her overstimulated heart to beat out a tattoo.

"You're here now." She made quite an effort to firm up her tone. God, he was a marvellous-looking man. She was coming to think of her attraction like a no-holds-barred thing, even as she knew it wasn't all chemical. At least having to look up at him was entirely satisfactory. Nine times out of ten she had to look down to make eye contact.

"So what have you been up to?" He came nonchalantly alongside, resting his lean, bronze arms on the white wrought-iron railing. An inch more and their fingers would touch. She could feel the blood in her veins turn to a thick golden syrup.

"I've been driving all around," she said, pleased she sounded almost normal. "I took in the polo fields. Worked out where I want to set up the tables and chairs for the spectators and the marquees. I have a favour to ask if you can manage it?"

"As long as it revolves around work." He glanced at her with mockery, thinking they were the right size for each other. Come live with me and be my love, his heart cried. Then he could go crazy with jealousy for the rest of his days.

She tilted her dimpled chin, dark eyes challenging. "What else, pray? I was thinking the ceiling of the Great Hall could do with a paint. Maybe cobalt-blue. I'd like to put a mural of sorts up there for the Polo Ball. I know just the guy who could do it."

"Another one of your admirers?" He couldn't help the taunt.

"As a matter of fact, yes. We're both creative."

"I bet! Then the answer's no." He was quite blunt.

"He's gay."

He pretended to find that bizarre when he felt a sense of relief. "Never! What did you have in mind?"

"I was thinking of stars."

He laughed shortly, wondering what it would be like making love beneath the stars.

"But then umbrellas came to mind."

"Where the hell did that come from?" His eyes were pure gold in the sun. His hair gleamed gold again against the black of his slouched hat.

"As in spectator brollies," she explained. "Floating silver cups and maybe a mallet or two."

"In which case wouldn't you colour the field green?" He glanced at her. "Polo is played on grass."

"Then you like the idea?" she said happily.

So happily he wanted to kiss her deeply. He wasn't used to happy women. Or women so charming they'd have you eating out of their hands. Despite that, he said, "Give me a minute. You've just thrown it at me."

"I think it would work well," she urged. "We'll carry out the polo theme. Maybe frame the dance floor like a pitch. Goal at either end."

"Why not an indoor match?"

"I thought indoor polo was gaining in popularity?"

"Not around here it isn't. We've got plenty of land. Plenty of sunshine. I was only being facetious."

"I realise that," she answered kindly. "I also want a beautiful big Christmas tree for the entrance hall. I want it to loft to the ceiling. All the lovely glittering baubles we can find. Like treasure chests spilling out Christmas angels. I want it to look—oh, magic!" She threw up her arms, irresistibly drawing his eyes to her full, beautiful breasts. Maybe that was the intention, he thought cynically. How formidable were females. And this was a volatile, passionate woman. Alas to a fault.

"And lots of beautifully wrapped presents piled beneath the tree." On her face was the excitement and wonder of a child. "I haven't as yet seen the guest list for the Christmas party but I imagine there will be children coming with their parents?"

"Quite a few, as it happens," he said, certain she was a woman who loved children. A woman children would love. Earthmother was written all over her. "You'll have to order up the tree, Angel," he said, using his new nickname for her. "We don't have any pines or spruce around here. A live tree would be too aromatic in the house."

"Leave it to me."

"I fully intend to. That's what you're here for." What would she do if he pulled her to him? The sudden urge was so drastic he had to refocus on that painful scene with Carly's rat of a husband. Even as he did he was forced to concede it was an out-and-out defence strategy. What the hell!

Angelica felt his abrupt change of mood. "Don't look like you want to throw me out," she said.

"Is that how it seems to you?" The flicker of desire in his amber eyes was so quick she doubted she saw it all.

"Either that or you want to eat me."

He laughed, a wonderfully attractive sound and a total departure from the edge of severity. "Undeniably you'd taste delicious. Are we going to get a forerunner of what you might be wearing at dinner?"

"Gracious, no. You have to wait for that." Her abundant hair was caught up at the back against the heat, but long curls spilled down onto the sides of her face and her nape. "I love it here," she said, holding his extraordinary eyes for just a moment. This man was dynamite. For the first time in her life she really didn't trust herself. She had read about men who took a woman's breath away but up until now she hadn't actually met one.

"You can't escape the heat." In a gesture quite beyond him to prevent, he reached out to push one glossy strand behind her ear.

"It does take a little getting used to." Excitement blossomed frantically. "It's a different heat altogether to what I'm used to." Heat, heat! What was he staring at? Could he see she was on fire?

"Ah, well, I'd better go take my shower," he said, as though tearing himself away. "Then I want a long cold beer."

"I can imagine." Her lips curved. "Actually a cold beer sounds good to me." She could see them clinking glasses.

He laughed, pushing his akubra down over his eyes as the last rays of the sun blitzed the verandah with gold. "Then

get Clary to organise something on the downstairs verandah.''

Angelica shook her head. "I won't bother Clary at all,"
she said. "She's cooking up something special for tonight. I
can handle drinks and a few nibbles without stopping our
appetite.''

"Then go to it, Angel," he advised. He started to move
off, already half drunk on her. What was her perfume?
Alluring femininity. She was a seriously beautiful woman
and he had seen her half naked. Probably seducing men was
the usual scenario for a siren like that. "Just give me half an
hour," he called back, sounding surprisingly light-hearted.

"Not a minute longer," she answered.

Captivating as she undoubtedly was, he didn't trust her.
Not one little inch. That could well be his problem, not hers.
All he really knew was it was astonishingly good to have her
under his roof.

CHAPTER FIVE

THE house looked splendid by night, giving Angelica a very good idea of what could be achieved for the Christmas party. The chandeliers were absolutely wonderful, antique but converted to electricity. Who had the job of cleaning them? she wondered with some awe. Clary and her girls? Or maybe Clary didn't trust the girls with the easily broken crystal. Whoever it was, Angelica didn't envy them the job. There were so many pieces to each it would take ages. But it was worth it. They cast their brilliance over the main entrance hall and the Yellow Drawing Room which, Stacy informed her, was rarely used except for special occasions, and the formal dining room which Angelica and Clary had decided they'd use that night even before knowing Gillian had invited the Honourable Charles Middleton to join them. Gillian had checked with Jake. It was all right. Did Angelica mind? Of course she didn't.

She was interested to meet the young aristocrat turned jackeroo, to discover, like Stacy, if his feelings for Gillian were encouraging or a result of fevered wishful thinking on Gillian's part. From what she'd seen of Gillian, admittedly very little, Angelica wasn't certain Gillian could handle serious hurt. From all accounts, this was Gillian's first taste of life after years of controlling by an authoritarian father. She was free and, according to her mother, in love. But Charlie came from another, much wider world.

She dressed for dinner in a style that really worked for her with her Latin looks. It could be described as Flamenco or gypsy. With her red, ankle-length flounced cotton voile skirt, she teamed a matching red top, V-necked and sleeveless, which was lovely and cool. A fancy gold belt to show off her narrow waist, long dangly earrings for a bit of chic, half a dozen bangles and a pair of her beloved very expensive high-heeled Italian gold sandals, which meant she was all of six feet. But what the heck! She'd accepted her height now. Even the wisecracks didn't jar so much.

When she went downstairs she checked in with Clary first. "How's it going? The kitchen smells wonderful."

"Everything organised," Clary reported, looking up from her preparations, highly pleased. "I'm loving this. It's quite a thrill cooking for someone who really understands food. Just don't slam me if something doesn't quite turn out."

"As if I'd do that," Angelica tutted. "This is going to be very successful, Clary, you'll see. Nothing too adventurous considering Stacy's and Gilly's delicate palates. We'll work up to that. Artichoke hearts with foie gras for starters, racks of lamb with a green herb crust, Moroccan orange tart. What more could they want? By the way, where's your help?"

"She'll be here in a moment." Clary adjusted her snowy apron around her ample waist. "She had to settle the little one, I expect."

"So it's Leah? Good, I can get to meet her."

She didn't have to wait long. A very slender young woman of exotic appearance with elegant, birdlike limbs, dressed in a stylish outfit with a fascinating ethnic print, came silently through the back door. Her dark skin had a high gloss. She had big, soft, gentle eyes. When she caught sight of Angelica she stood perfectly still for a moment, but Clary called to her in an encouraging voice. "Come on in, Leah. Meet Miss De Campo. I told you all about her."

Leah walked slowly across the room as though she had a heavy jar on her head, her dark eyes on Angelica standing so dramatically in her red dress that threw off vibrant light. "Hello, Leah." Angelica put out her hand, smiling at the woman. The slender hand was like a living bird's, trembling faintly. She put Angelica in mind of a small vulnerable creature of the wild ready to take off at the slightest breath of alarm. "I'm so pleased to meet you. I love the outfit you're wearing. I'd like to wear something like that myself."

"Then I'll make something for you," the young woman announced softly, apparently having made up her mind Angelica was a friend. "It's hand-painted to my own design."

"It's beautiful." Angelica, very fashion conscious, took a closer look. "You must be a very good dress-maker, as well," she concluded, impressed.

"Learned it off the nuns she did," Clary supplied. "Mission school. Natural talent. 'Course the nuns couldn't teach her how to do all her lovely prints. That's her world. The dreaming. Painting and drawing is your heritage, isn't it, Leah?"

"Yes," Leah agreed simply.

"We'll have to talk more about this, Leah," Angelica said with some enthusiasm, but aware there was work to be done. "I'd love to see more of what you do. You wear your own designs beautifully. You could have been a model walking across the room. I expect you know, quite a few indigenous designers are making it in the fashion world. There's a showing heading to Italy right now. I'm of Italian descent."

"You're beautiful!" Leah pronounced, pressing a finger to a spot between her brows as though therein lay a third eye. There were no waves of anger or venom around this woman as tall as a queen. Leah with her sad background was very careful about people. "I could make something to please you," she said, studying Angelica's body intently. "I know your size."

"Just like that?" Angelica laughed.

"Just like that." Leah nodded, looking up to meet Angelica's smiling eyes. "You could wear my clothes. Not everyone can."

"See, you're one of the lucky ones, Angelica," Clary said. "Now come on, Leah, no more chatting, we've got work to do."

''It's just like the convent.'' Leah flashed Angelica a white grin, bright little sparks of mischief in her melancholy eyes.

When Angelica walked into the splendid drawing room with gilt stucco work on the ceiling and around a pair of very beautiful gilt mirrors almost the size of the wall, she found Jake staring up at the portrait of his mother. For a moment she hesitated to approach him, sensitive to the feelings that surrounded Roxanne. What was he thinking of? Loss? How beautiful she was? How much he resembled her? How very different his life would have been had she lived? It must have taken a lot of inner strength to have survived his harsh up-bringing with his spirit intact.

She was just about to retreat when he turned abruptly, his brilliant amber eyes moving over her from head to toe. ''What took you so long?''

She answered with comic gravity. ''You'll have to learn patience, Mr. McCord. Actually I wanted to have a word with Clary.''

''Ah, yes!'' He turned to face her squarely, his mother's painted image for a backdrop.

What a piece of work is man, Angelica thought, lost in admiration. He looked stunning in a collarless cream linen shirt and deeper-toned trousers, the light colour playing up his dark golden skin and bronzed hair.

''Clary's as taken with you as my stepmother and sister,'' he told her as though she may have developed a practised charm instead of inheriting it in the cradle.

''So tell me, are you feeling better about me?'' she asked, with a little challenging smile.

''The points are going up,'' he assured her. ''I know I love that dress.''

''Why thank you.'' She dropped a perfectly balanced little curtsy.

''Are you going to dance for us later?'' he asked suavely, his eyes alive with mockery.

''You mean, flamenco?''

"You are sporting that personality surely?"

"Gypsy's in," she told him airily. "It works for me. Actually I'm more interested in one of your employees."

"Oh, hell no!" He turned about.

"Why do you say that?" she asked in astonishment.

"I guess I'll just have to wait for you to tell me."

"Listen, it's Leah," she said. "Leah helps Clary in the kitchen."

"Why thank you for that helpful piece of information, Miss De Campo. I do know Leah."

"Okay, okay, you don't give me much of a chance. Leah is very gifted. She was wearing an outfit that I'd fancy wearing myself."

"See if she'll sell it to you," he suggested sardonically.

"You don't understand." She clicked her teeth in exasperation. "She designed and made it herself. She's good. I know about these things."

"I'm prepared to believe that. I've never seen anyone with so much oomph."

"Can I help it?" she countered. "The thing is, I'd really like to do something for her."

"I'm not going to stop you," he answered mildly. "Leah needs help. She's lived a hard life."

"And you rescued her?" She loved him for being kind.

"My God, years too late!" He sounded angry the young aboriginal woman had had to suffer so much pain and distress. "You'll know from Clary she has a child."

"Kylee. At least she has someone to love," Angelica said thankfully, moving to where he stood, again experiencing a sensuous arousal that was becoming familiar. "Your mother was a glorious-looking woman," she ventured gently, looking up at the painted golden eyes as she had not been invited to before.

"Spoken by a woman who could pass for Venus?"

"You think so?" A little pulse was beating up a storm in her throat.

"Oh, for God's sake, you know you're beautiful," he said almost roughly.

"Why do you make that sound like it's just another thing you hate about me?" Provoked, her reaction was nearly as fierce as his. He was such an unpredictable man.

"I'm just worried you're going to use it on me."

"On you?" she asked with scorn. "I'd have my work cut out."

"That wouldn't stop you trying."

"In another minute I'm going to slap you," she warned, a non-violent woman aroused.

"What did I tell you? You're a real powerhouse," he scoffed, unperturbed.

"You're not exactly…normal, either." Not with all those hard, glittery edges.

"And what is your definition of normal, my Angel?" he asked, looking so deeply into her eyes her mind spun. "A man who falls instantly under your spell?"

She tried to hold his amber gaze as long as she could without actually drowning. "You're the most arrogant man I know," she muttered.

"You've already figured that out." His expression softened miraculously, became almost indulgent. "Why any minute now we'll have a full-blown argument. Our first. I'm sorry. My mother did teach me manners. You're not exactly a guest, but you're under my roof."

"And I have my reputation to think about." She turned her attention back to the portrait, staring up at the lovely, luminous face. "You remember her well?"

"I remember some things very clearly. My father was different then. It was the suffering that made him bitter."

"It must help you to understand that," she said. "It would have been terrible for him to lose the young wife he adored. And in such a way."

"One of the worst things in life," he answered sombrely.

"And for you to lose your mother," she added, thinking how it must have been for a small thoughtful child.

"I survived," he told her in a closed-off voice. "Nothing like a touch of the whip to keep you on course."

"It couldn't have been so easy for Stacy and Gillian, either." She was acutely aware of the tension in him. "Women can sometimes seem so much more vulnerable to the lack of love."

"You appear to know a whole lot about my family."

She coloured at his tone. "People have a tendency to confide in me."

"You think I might fit into that category?"

"How could you when you don't even have a basic trust?"

"True." The golden-amber eyes traced a course over her face, throat, to the swell of her breasts. "How did you finally get rid of Trevor?" he asked very softly. Too softly.

She shivered. "I sent my brother Bruno along to explain the situation. I think I told you, Bruno is six-six."

"Yes. That's over my head." He gave an appreciative laugh. "What does Bruno do?"

"He's spectacularly talented like me. He's a sports commentator. He's on TV. He's great-looking."

"I can well believe that. Italians are a very handsome people and you show your heritage."

"A heritage I'm very proud of. When we were kids people used to think we were twins. Anyway, Bruno put the fear of God into Trevor."

"So how did you get involved in the first place?" he asked so abruptly he might have wished to trip her up.

"I told you, but you don't want to believe it."

He shrugged a wide shoulder. "Oh, I want to believe it, Angel, but I really require a little more than your maidenly protestations."

"Your cynicism knows no bounds. Why exactly? Why are you so wary of women or is it just me? Why are you being judge, jury and executioner?"

"In all likelihood I want you to be as good as you're beautiful," he surprised himself by admitting out loud. "To answer your question, I don't exactly know why I'm so hard on you. And it is you. I've never been like this before. Maybe it was the way I was raised." He looked back up at the portrait of his mother. "I never got the chance to know my mother well. All I've had is a portrait of a beautiful woman, forever young, and a few precious memories. I've idealised her so I guess I see a woman who moves me in those terms. Can you understand any of that?"

The seriousness, even the strange appeal in his expression, made her tremble. "Yes I can. You've put your mother up on a pedestal and you expect the woman you want to occupy that lofty position, as well. That presents a dilemma when life is full of pitfalls."

"So you're saying even a woman of honourable intentions can be led astray?" He hated the suavity in his own voice, the cutting edge, when God knows he wasn't what he really intended.

"You can't eradicate Huntley from your mind, can you?" she said, almost sorrowfully. "Probably in the wake of such a dysfunctional childhood and adolescence you back away from powerful attachments. Any excuse might do. The very fact you're not married—"

He held up a lean hand. "Stop trying to push the buttons. You're not here to tell me how to live my life."

"I'm trying to help you." She laid a hesitant hand on his arm. "Moreover I'm trying to help myself. We should be able to talk it over. I don't want one unsavoury incident to spoil any friendship that might be possible between us. But you give me the impression you think I'm the sort of woman who might hurt you."

"Cut me to ribbons?" Unexpectedly, as though she were a princess, he lifted her hand, barely brushing a kiss on her silky skin. Then his velvety eyelids came down heavily over his big cat's eyes. "We've talked enough about me, Angel. You can try to redeem me if you like."

At his touch excitement raged through her. "It's a challenge!" she admitted huskily, seeing the dare in his shimmering glance. A glorious challenge! But was she ready to take it on?

Very slowly, he put a finger to the shallow dimple in her chin. "And you've a high rate of success."

"What do you want to hear?" She stared back at him, willing her heart to settle. "I've had plenty?"

I don't want another man touching you, he thought, his expression turning stormy. She was so beautiful, that abundant hair flowing around her face and over her shoulders. Her eyes were as dark as night but when she laughed they were filled with little flickering stars. He wanted to kiss her deeply, lavishly, with all the passion that beat in his blood.

"I never believed in a witch until I met you," he said, thinking what it would be like to keep her forever.

"Yet you still call me Angel? I have to tell you no one else has called me that." It seemed important to bring the fact to his attention. "You need to think about that, Jake McCord. Because I can't be both."

The Honourable Charles Middleton turned out to be a very charming young man, carefully dressed for the occasion in a long-sleeved blue shirt with a blue-and-navy-striped tie and jeans that sat neatly on his lanky six-foot frame. He had floppy blond sun-streaked hair, and his fine English skin was perfectly tanned. His eyes in contrast were a heavenly blue. He stared at Angelica, an incredulous expression in those eyes, as if she were a sight he hadn't been prepared for. "Delighted to meet you, Miss De Campo," he said enthusiastically, as if he wouldn't have missed meeting her for the world.

That earned him a hurt look from Gillian, only as he wasn't looking in her direction he missed it.

Jake didn't. Not that he was terribly surprised. Angel was enough to distract any man.

They found their way into the dining room, Charlie exclaiming how delightful it was to be dining there. Usually the family used the smaller informal dining room overlooking the large swimming pool Jake had decided to put in. Angelica had seen it that very afternoon, amazed by the great profusion of blossoming bougainvillea spilling over the roof of the stone pool house.

"This room has such perfect proportions," Charlie said, lifting his blond head. "It reminds me a little of the dining room at home. I expect it's the decorated ceiling and the panels on the walls."

"Now then, Charlie, you know the dining room at home is at least twice as big," Jake said dryly.

"Well it was the banquet hall at one time." Charlie gave him a quick, boyish grin. "There's an immense fireplace in the drawing room. My sister and I used to think it looked like a tomb."

"You must miss home, Charles?" Angel asked. Although his name had been cut to Charlie, he was actually much more a Charles in her opinion.

"Oh I do, but I love it here. As someone from a small country, it fascinates me. Australia is so vast. One can travel for days and still be in the same state."

Gillian held out her hand. "You must sit beside me, Charlie."

"Yes of course," Charles agreed at once, smiling almost conspiratorially at Angelica.

Dinner went wonderfully well. Charles was an easy conversationalist. He had read widely, travelled widely and was very intelligent. He didn't seem to be attaching the same significance to their friendship as Gilly was, Angelica thought with a little lurch of dismay. The station was so isolated Gilly had little chance of meeting and mixing with eligible young men. Small wonder she had fallen so hard for the handsome Charles.

Leah brought in the entrees, serving quietly and efficiently, giving Angelica a little over-the-shoulder smile as she left to return to the kitchen.

"Does she really have to wear a dress like that?" asked Gillian.

"I love it." Angelica looked up, surprised. "Don't you?"

"I think a uniform would be more suitable. Father would have insisted she wear one."

"Don't let his snobbery wear off on you, Gilly." Jake spoke quietly, aware his half sister had picked up some of their father's more sorry traits.

"Actually she's a very interesting and charming woman." Without realising, Charles added fuel to the fire. "She paints, as well, adding to her gifts. I've bought a few of her paintings. She sells them for a song. I'm very drawn to them. She uses such vivid, stylised patterns, which obviously mean something."

"They go far beyond decoration," Jake added. "The designs are important. They represent, symbolically, the great ancestral and mythical beings. What I noticed of the design of the dress she has on was magic in nature."

"Really?" Angelica was fascinated, turning her dark head to look straight into his amber eyes. She wanted him to continue but she was aware of Gillian's discomfort.

Gillian cut in, looking stunned. "You've bought paintings off Leah?" She rounded on Charles as though the news had shattered her.

"Gilly, I've often told you how talented Leah is," Jake said quickly, trying to head her off. "You can't have been listening."

"Probably you should look at Leah's paintings yourself, Gilly." Charles tapped Gillian's wrist in a series of rapid, gentle movements. "She'll show you if you ask nicely."

"I don't intend to ask at all." Gillian all but turned up her pert nose.

"Your loss." Charles laughed it off. "I bet she'd show them to you, Angelica." He looked at Angelica across the gleaming table, a bright light in his blue eyes.

"I'd really enjoy that. She's already promised me she'd make me a dress." Angelica looked to Gillian to smile, but there was no smile back. Oh dear, she thinks I'm trying to steal her boyfriend. How unfortunate. Gilly didn't realise there was a man in her life already. A man who made Charles look like a charming boy.

"You wouldn't wear it, would you, dear?" Stacy turned a surprised face.

"Of course I would." The "course" soared in surprise. She really didn't understand Stacy's and Gillian's patronising attitude, which seemed odd to her.

"You've got taste," the egalitarian Charles said, as though that settled it. "You'll look marvellous in it. You have the style to carry off the look. And the dramatic colouring." He put down his knife and fork to steeple his fingers, sitting back in his chair to consider her like a sculpture.

"For what it's worth," Jake said dryly. "I agree. So now we all have something to look forward to. Angelica in her new dress. Probably the symbols will have something to do with woman-magic."

"Oh, I love that!" Charles exclaimed delightedly.

Clary ushered in the main course, which went down very well. "This is absolutely delicious!" Charles gasped, rolling the word on his tongue. "I understand you and Clary put your heads together on the menu, Angelica?"

"Well…" Angelica caught Gillian's sulk and nearly moaned. "Clary did the actual cooking."

"I know you're marvellous, too." Charles seemed quite unaware his little pleasantries were being interpreted by Gillian and her protective mother as unacceptable gush. "I must try to get copies of *Cosima* magazine. I'd love to read your features."

"You're not in need of a husband, are you, Angelica?" Jake quipped lightly at Charlie's expense.

"What, you of all people proposing?" In turn she mocked him, tilting her chin with its provocative dimple.

"Charlie's the one who's getting carried away."

Stacy and Gillian looked at him blankly. "You're joking, aren't you, dear?" Stacy questioned finally.

"Of course I am," he gently teased, thinking Gilly might have to be brought down to earth a bit. Even so, it wasn't the moment to point out Angelica had scored big with the Honourable Charles. Even the way she said his name was having an effect on the effervescent Charlie, much like a glass of champagne.

By the time they finished dessert, the air was literally electric. The heaviness of the impending storm continued while all rain held off. Violent thunder rocked back and forth. Once the great chandeliers dimmed as lightning zigzagged across the sky with a blinding white metallic flash that lit up the long windows.

Angelica jumped in her seat, setting her dangly earrings in motion. "Gosh, this weather is making me very nervous."

To her surprised delight Jake stretched out a reassuring hand to her, touching her bare skin. "Don't let it frighten you." Heat and power flowed from him to her. She thought he could cure her if she were ill.

Afterwards Gillian, a certain determined look in her eye, bore Charles off to hear CDs that had just arrived.

"I'm so sleepy after that wonderful meal I'll probably listen with only half an ear," said Charles.

Not the most lover-like of statements, Jake thought, figuring he would have to review his assessment of the relationship based a lot on hearsay from Gilly that could be little more than feverish wishful thinking.

Stacy might have been reviewing matters, as well. She excused herself, obviously in a bit of a tizzy, saying she had a few little jobs to do without volunteering exactly what they were.

"What do you say we go for a walk?" A bit rattled himself, Jake sought Angelica's satiny bare arm.

"You're asking me to brave the storm?" She stared up at him thinking she would probably go with him to rob a bank.

"It's not a storm. It's a circus out there." Inside, as well, he thought.

"I've been waiting all my life to be hit by lightning," she informed him laconically.

He looked down at her vivid face. Red was her colour.

The colour of passion. Some mouths although not overfull were wonderfully voluptuous. He had a sudden desire to put his hands around her lovely, long throat, thumbs tilting up her chin… "Come on," he said abruptly. "We'll stay on the verandah. But I want a breath of fresh air."

Outside in the night she inhaled the ozone. Great eucalypts reared to either side of the house, branches swishing with the urgency of the wind.

"How would you describe Charlie?" he asked, coming to stand beside her. The long skirt of her dress rippled and twisted around her long legs. Her hair blew free, streaming out behind her. Her profile looked carved.

"Let me see." She turned towards him then laughed when her hair suddenly streamed around her face. "I like him. There's a certain sweetness about him. And he's really classy. Am I getting warm?"

"I'm looking for an answer. To put it bluntly, he was very taken with you."

"Is that an additional sin?" She was stung to defend herself, wondering if it was always going to be like this. "I thought he was just being pleasant."

"Pleasant and very responsive," he said dryly. "What I'm trying to get at is—and after this evening I'm confused—is he romantically interested in Gilly?"

Angel feared he wasn't. Well, not all that much. "Maybe I'm as confused as you are," she evaded.

"I don't think so. You know men."

"Please don't use Trevor Huntley again as an illustration."

"Forget him." Being so near to her was like sinking his head into a bowl of gorgeous red roses coming into full bloom. Somehow, God help him, she ignited the poet in him. Nevertheless he clipped off, "I have a family to protect."

"Gilly has to learn her own lessons," she bravely offered.

"So what are you saying? You don't think Charlie is in love with her?"

"I'm sure he enjoys her company," she said diplomatically. "We all want a bit of excitement in our lives. Gilly is a pretty girl. She could be even prettier with a little help. I'd love to take her shopping. I know exactly how she can bring out her best points.''

He groaned, stepping back. ''Oh, great! Are you sure you shouldn't get into the beauty business?''

''Looking good is my business,'' she said tartly. ''As for Charles…''

''Isn't that darling…Charles.'' He made an excellent job of mimicking her honeyed tones. So good she didn't take offence.

''I must say that's terribly good. Some people say there's a layer of Italian in my accent. You got it just right. Anyway, he is a Charles, isn't he? Not a Charlie. Apart from the fact he's an Honourable—whatever that means—he's simply not the kind of young man one calls Charlie.''

He gave a scoffing laugh. ''Tell that to the boys down at the stockmen's quarters. At least it's better than Charlie the Pom. That's all he got when he arrived.''

''Goodness, what are you people?'' she asked sternly.

Surprisingly he smiled lazily. ''Just having a bit of fun. Charlie stuck it out like the good sport he is. Now they all laugh together.''

''Sadly for Gilly, I think Charles will go home,'' she predicted, staring out into the wild night like she was seeing into the future. ''Probably when he's satisfied his sense of adventure.''

''I told you that,'' he reminded her sarcastically. ''He can't have fallen in love with Gilly if he was so easily taken with you.''

''Ah, then, but I'm a real stunner even if you're indifferent.'' She turned the sarcasm back on him. ''Seriously, and I could be wrong, I think Gilly is in love with love. She can't manage to meet many young men when she lives way out here at the back of beyond. She must be longing for affection.''

''She gets affection.'' His amber eyes turned electric.

She'd have to take a touch more care. "No need to snap my head off," she protested.

"Pardon me. I've spent more time apologising to you than anyone I can think of."

"I don't think you've spent much time apologising to anyone." Having spoken her piece, she bit her lip.

"Shouldn't you mention my arrogance again?"

"Wouldn't it be a good idea if we tried to be friends?"

"I thought we were really good friends already," he said, subjecting her to another flashing look.

"Nope." She shook her wind-tossed dark curls. "We're not. We might have been only for a single incident three years ago."

"You mean, Carly's husband trying to make violent love to you." He gave a hoot of derision.

"I was raised in a good Christian environment. You just can't admit it's possible to be tricked." Even as she spoke, her anger turned to simple shock. She looked up at the sky, one hand rising to her cheek. "Isn't that a drop of rain?"

He slumped back against a white vine-wreathed pillar. "My poor girl, we haven't had rain for a year."

"I'm not stupid, you know. That's a spit of rain. There there's another one." She felt a great wave of something like joy. "Feel!" She moved over to him, holding up her face for his touch.

"You've been crying," he gently mocked, just barely suppressing his desire to put his hand around her narrow waist and draw her into his arms. What skin she had! God, it was like satin. She was intoxicating. So intoxicating he allowed his hand to drift over her cheek, the tips of his fingers full of sensation. "Is this another one of your little tricks?" he asked, coming dangerously close to breaking loose.

"Damn it, Jake." His touch made her turbulent, shattering what poise she had left. "There it is again. Has it got to pelt down before you take any notice?"

He dropped his hand abruptly, refocussing, his nostrils assailed by a new element in the air. Thunder cracked again,

splitting open the whole world. A great silver blade of lightning buried itself in the red earth. He was used to this climatic phenomena. He had lived with it all his life. Mostly it
was spectacular pyrotechnics resulting in not a single drop
of rain. Only this time it was different.

"Fantastic!" Angelica leaned over the balustrade, inhaling
deeply the uniquely fresh, subtle perfume of rain. The drops
came heavier onto her face, onto the top of the tongue she
put out to catch them. She closed her eyes in a kind of rapture. This was what this vast parched Inland craved. Water.

Soon it wasn't enough to stand on the verandah. She had
to seize the moment. She stopped only seconds to remove
her beautiful expensive sandals then she ran down the low
flight of stone steps, calling to Jake over her shoulder, "This
is what you want, isn't it?"

Rainwater was streaming over her hair, her forehead and
cheeks, down her throat, between her breasts, down over her
long cotton voile skirt to her bare feet. Rain, rain, rain! After
the heat it was bliss!

But Jake continued to stand on the verandah, leaning hard
against the white pillar, hypnotised by the sight of her. She
was doing some kind of little rain dance, rivulets of water
glittering all over her, causing her red dress to closely mould
her body. It almost tore the heart from him. He could feel
his sensual response to her in every nerve, every muscle,
every fibre. Despite his odd ambivalence, he wanted to go to
her, crush her to him, mindless of the inevitable complica-
tions. He wanted to hold up her face to him, kiss that luscious, alluring mouth. He wanted to hear her moan his name.
Not Jake. Jonathon. He wanted to hear his name again after
all these years. Unparalleled in his experience, he wanted this
woman. He wanted to kiss every inch of her naked, delectable, pliant flesh.

Getting soaking wet didn't concern her in the least. Her
graceful movements, incredibly erotic to his eyes, began to
change. Incredible! She had moved into a different kind of
dance, a gypsy flamenco with its unique heart-stirring steps.

"Just for you," she called, lifting her long beautiful arms above her head while she stamped her bare feet on the glistening earth. She was the very image of a beautiful, seductive gypsy woman, confident in her powerful allure, indeed glorying in it, while he stood before her spellbound.

Then like a miracle, as if she read his every desire, she cried out to him breathlessly, "Jonathon, what are you doing up there? Come to me. It's so wonderful!"

He needed no further invitation, his passions inflamed. His strong tanned hands clenched and unclenched. How had she known to call him Jonathon? Was it possible this woman dabbled in magic? He believed now that certain women down the ages were capable of witchcraft.

He came to her as sleekly, as powerfully, as a big cat. It even had a hint of violence in it, as though he were responding to something primitive in him. He was vaguely aware the rain was coming down heavier now. But his need to take hold of this woman was so overwhelming it became his sole interest. When he reached her, hauling her to him, his hands on her shoulders, they both gasped with the shock and excitement of it, stumbling backwards until they were totally obscured by the great golden canes, tremulously singing some kind of wind song.

Their fronds parted to contain and cocoon them as he folded her tight into his body, silencing her little jagged gasps as he took her lush mouth.

It was an explosion of desire such as he had never known. An assuagement of some deep permanent hunger. His hands were bold. They went where they wanted. To her beautiful breasts, almost too womanly, too voluptuous, for a man to bear, the nipples tight as berries, inviting the further stimulation of his fingers. He wanted her, nothing more, nothing less. He was holding her to him, his left hand locked strongly to her back. Her long dress was so wet, so slick against her body, he could have peeled it from her.

Either the kiss had gone on and on or he was kissing her again while she arched against him, mouth open, body yield-

ing as though his sudden onslaught had gained him total do-
minion. When he finally came halfway to his senses, he
jerked back his head, letting his hands fall to her golden hips.
They were surrounded by a wilderness of wet greenery and
silver rain and the heady fragrance released from the beds of
white lilies that grew beneath the trees. Little tremors were
flickering through his arms. He craved this woman. This
purely dangerous woman who could inspire so much rapture.
The rain was still falling. Real rain pouring out of the sky.
He had never known anything like it The wild improbability
of it all! For a woman never lost for a word, she was very
quiet, weakened perhaps by the powerful momentum of his
desire, as stormy and tumultuous as the elements.

"Are you all right? Tell me," he muttered, his voice deep-
ened by emotion, his arm still tight around her.

But Angelica was reeling from the power of the feeling
he'd unleashed. Strangely, when she no longer was, she felt
like a virgin only just awakened to the full blinding rush of
physical passion.

"Angel, why you?" he asked in a dark, near melancholy
voice.

That released her. Slowed the wild beating of her heart.

"Because I'm here?" She threw up her expressive head
to challenge him. A tall woman with her own tensile strength.

"You are." A flame jumped back and forth between them
that could not be extinguished by rain, caution, or lack of
trust. "And it's magic!" He pressed a finger into the hollow
of her rain-slicked neck. The pulse was hammering. He left
his finger there hoping that through her pulse he could hold
on to her heart.

All hostility seemed to drain away. "The rain tastes
sweet," she whispered. "Isn't that strange?"

"Nothing's strange with you." He spread his long tanned
fingers over her throat, dipping his head so he could run his
tongue over her wet cheek, gathering up the delicious mois-
ture. His vibrant voice was almost dreamy. "I want to make
love to you, you know that?"

Yes, oh yes! She thought blindly. Tonight. For the longest, longest time. Until dawn. Everything about him called to her like a voice she was programmed to obey. Now his mouth brushed against her sensitive neck, moving back and forth.

Excitement flowed into her so she was near oblivious to the streaming rain and the pungent steam that rose from the hot earth and the tiled walkways. Tendrils of wet curls fell on her brow and her cheeks like ribbons of silk. The paradox of it all! She felt marvellously safe within his arms, and yet endangered, knowing full well this man could reach in and steal her heart.

"Jonathon, it's so sudden," she murmured, as his mouth sought hers again. "Sexual attraction can't be all there is." Even as she protested, that same attraction was pushing her to the edge.

"Why Jonathon?" he demanded urgently. "Whatever prompted you to call me that? And why now? Are you mocking me?"

She was shocked he might think so. "But your name is Jonathon. Isobel told me it was your father who renamed you Jake."

"And you suddenly remembered?"

"Stop it." She lifted a hand to his mouth as if to silence him. "If you don't want me to call you Jonathon, I won't."

She sounded so upset he found himself full of remorse, cradling her. "Hushhhhhhh... I do like it," he told her tenderly. "You have a gift." It was so wonderful he couldn't properly interpret it. He could only recognise there was far more to what had passed between them than a man's driving passion and need for release. He wanted to mate with this woman. He wanted to take her to bed. At that moment he couldn't care less about old indiscretions.

Except that wasn't entirely true. He wanted her to be utterly faithful. To him. He wasn't fully aware of the extent of his needs. He only knew she was very, very special. And there was something else he was forced to consider. Once he let her into his heart she could very easily go away. He knew all about loss.

Sweet God, he had to be out of his mind. He stepped back so quickly Angelica staggered and had to clutch at his soaked shirt. "We have to get you out of this wet gear," he muttered, trying to dispel the tremendous build-up of intimacy between them with a certain curtness of tone. The skin of her face, throat and arms was shimmering with the lustre of a golden South Sea pearl. It seemed a whole lifetime had passed while they were cocooned together amid the storm-tossed palms. Time out of mind.

On the path she began to shiver and he pulled her drenched figure to him, angling his head and body so he was protecting her from the silver, slanting rain. "Are you cold?"

"A little bit." She knew it was a reaction to the loss of his body heat.

"We'll go in by the rear staircase. I'm astounded no one has come out to greet our small miracle. Maybe they're on the verandah."

The rain that had so passionately cracked down turned off like a tap. By the time they stumbled into the rear hall with the wind hammering at their backs it seemed to be all over. They could hear the sound of laughter coming from somewhere upstairs then rapturous clapping.

"That's them!" Jake said, looking down at the puddles of water at their feet. "Stay here for a moment. I'll grab a few towels. Better yet we'll try the first-aid room." He ushered her down the polished cedar-wood hallway to a doorway on the right. He lifted his hand and the light snapped on, revealing a large, white-tiled room with a high bed like those one saw in a doctor's room, and rows of glass-fronted white cabinets holding an array of medical things.

"You really should get that dress off," he said, his gaze going over her. In the glare from the fluorescent lights she still managed to look stunning, soaked to the skin, even though she'd gone from seductive gypsy to drenched woman, her gleaming hair separating into long ebony curls.

"The towel will have to do," she said, shaking her hair back and scattering spray. "I'm not really cold. It's a reaction."

"It wasn't what you were expecting," he said, a little raggedly, walking away to a cupboard and taking out a pair of large white towels. "Here, catch."

Instantly she held up her hands like the athlete she'd been. "Got it."

He laughed as some of the tension was cut, using a towel on himself. "Another one for your hair." This time he located a hand towel, but instead of tossing it to her as before he came to stand behind her, gathering up her long hair to dry it.

"No need!" She was quivering and breathless standing so close, aware how terribly exciting he was to her.

"But I want to." His voice was exquisitely gentle, doubly sensual because of it. "Go ahead, wrap yourself in that towel."

She obeyed, slinging the towel around her hips, sarong-style. "What would you say is your real problem with me?" she asked, wishing and wishing they hadn't started off so badly.

"You make me confused," he said with a fine edge of despair, bending his head and kissing her shoulder, then moving the neck of her dress to kiss the other. "Why aren't you married, beautiful Angelica? A woman like you with this mane of black silk. It's superb."

"Why aren't you?" she countered, thinking she had never known such a wide range of sensations.

"I've never met a woman who possessed magic."

"And I've never met the right man. Not one who could offer me more than passing pleasure."

"You mean no dangerous rapture?" He turned her to face the wall mirror, the difference in their colouring startling.

"Isn't that what we all want, after all?" she asked wistfully.

"And seldom get. Even then there's a price."

His eyes were glittering like wonderful topaz, the kind of stones princes of old used to keep for themselves. Neither of them moved. Neither of them seemingly capable of fighting out of their emotional bounds.

A laughing English voice suddenly echoed through the hallway, releasing them instantly. "I say, you two. Where are you?"

"Here, Charlie," Jake called. "The first-aid room."

"Good grief! Everything okay?" Charlie appeared in the open doorway, his look of concern turning into one of enjoyment. "You've been out in the pouring rain. Isn't that exactly what I wanted. I was mad to tear down the stairs only Gilly didn't want to get wet. Some Aussie she is when she shudders at life in the great outdoors."

"Hi, Charlie," Jake said.

"Not intruding, am I?" Now Charlie sounded a little awkward.

"Believe me, you are. Angelica and I were considering whether we should top off the evening by making violent love," Jake told him dryly.

"What!" Charlie near choked, wedging himself against the door in shock, even if Jake had used a light satiric tone. "I suppose it is almost the night for it."

"He's joking, Charles." Angelica calmed him. "Far more important to get dry. But that was a marvellous downpour. Hasn't it cooled the air!"

"And so unexpected." Charlie was fascinated by Angel's appearance, more gypsy-ish than ever and marvellously sexy. He had never seen a woman look like that in the rain before. "We've had storm-clouds darkening the sky night after night." He looked to Jake. "Heavens knows what happened tonight. A meteorologist could explain it. Usually it all goes away. Now this!"

"A miracle! Here's to our Christmas Angel," Jake said suavely, with an elegant bow in Angelica's direction. "Angelica De Campo. A woman like no other."

"I'll second that!" Charlie's voice was saturated with boyish enthusiasm.

One stormy night on Coori station and her whole life had changed course.

CHAPTER SIX

SHE was awake at first light, fascinated by the sounds of the birds. Never in her life had she heard such a glorious din. Indeed the birdsong was so loud, so sweetly piercing, she found it impossible to stay in bed. She had been given what was virtually a suite, a huge bedroom, dominated by a marvellous four-poster with carved columns—Stacy had told her Jake's great-grandfather had brought it back from India along with many other pieces of furniture and artifacts in the house. The bed was hung with ivory voile to keep out insects.

There was an adjoining bathroom that was very Victorian in its splendour—a lion-clawed bath, rich dark timberwork, rose-trellised leadlight window. On the other side of the bedroom there was a pretty sitting room-study. Now she threw back the sheer hangings, which gave her such a sense of fantasy, and swung her feet to the carpeted floor. The light was increasing. Golden rays were cutting through the pearl-grey and lemon. She had slept soundly as though those long minutes of aching passion had weakened her to the point that all she could do was sleep to regain her strength.

He hadn't come to her room. She didn't know what she would have done if he had. Exactly the same thing as had happened when they were lost in the storm? She was convinced the storm had been the propellant. It had the quality of magic about it. It had stirred her to dance in front of him, in a way that must have seemed related to a dance of seduction. Whatever it was, it had electrified him, making him for a short time lose control. But there had been other emotions merged with his desire. She had felt them. Apprehension? Remembered pain? The terrible pain when his mother had been ripped out of his life? A subconscious desire never to go through that pain again? Or the thought of one humiliating moment out of time he couldn't let go of. She even had to consider that other woman who had hurt him years ago and forever made him wary. Jake was, after all, a man of deep feelings.

Sighing quietly, Angel walked out onto the wide balcony. She hadn't bothered to put on her robe. It was dawn. Who would be around? The front of the house overlooked a great expanse of lawn, trees and circular gardens, all fed by bore water. The homestead by everyday standards was enormous. She thought it would take her weeks to get around it. Built of rosy bricks, it presented the formality and symmetry of a Georgian building set down in the vast, timeless grandeur of the Outback. It was two-storied with deep verandahs supported by soaring white columns all vine-wreathed with a beautiful mauve flower. The rooms were set out in line across the facade, with main reception rooms downstairs, bedrooms up, all rooms fitted with white-painted French doors and frosty-white decorative ironwork to enclose the surrounding verandahs. It was a splendid house that must have conjured up nostalgic memories of the homeland and the old life that was missed, all the more extraordinary because of its wild, remote setting.

It had seemed to her as she'd been shown through the house that while the furnishings, Persian rugs and paintings were magnificent, some refurbishing was in order. Money to bring in expert interior designers didn't appear to be the problem. Obviously Stacy had decided to leave well enough alone. Maybe she needed some encouragement. Jake—why had she been inspired to call him Jonathon last night? Was some spirit voice prompting her? She really didn't know— couldn't be expected to take on domestic matters when he had a huge enterprise to run. Had she been one of the McCord women she wouldn't have hesitated to have a go. New curtains for the Yellow Drawing Room would make a difference. The ones that were, though they must have been splendid when they first went up, had been allowed to fade, their golden radiance dimmed.

She realised with some amusement she was the sort of woman who was always looking to improve her surroundings. If she hadn't gotten into the food business, she would liked to have been an interior designer. That was her artistic streak. Her mother always said she had one. At least dinner last night had been a minor triumph. The master of the house, hungry after a long day's work, and his surprisingly privileged jackeroo had little difficulty polishing it off, their appreciation evident. Even Stacy and Gilly, usually light eaters, had found everything satisfying.

As she approached the wrought-iron balustrade, her satin nightdress falling opalescent around her, the horizon was suddenly gilded by a great ball of fire. Kookaburras broke into their demented cackling, a sound, nevertheless that touched her heart. She drew in a deep breath of air washed clean by that marvellous downpour of rain then lifted her arms above her, stretching...stretching...rising up onto her toes. She had just about redesigned her body over the last two years going to the gym. Now she couldn't help knowing she had a great body, but it hadn't come easily. Let's face it, she had to stick with the program and watch her diet when she was surrounded by abundant, delicious food. Of course she and Bruno broke out from time to time especially when they went over to their parents' for Sunday brunch.

A man's voice called to her. "If you bent over right now I bet you could touch your toes."

Her flush was merciless, staining her cheeks. Immediately she arched back, dropping her arms, hoping he couldn't see through her nightdress. To counter that, she stepped away from the balustrade, lest she be caught in the sun's early rays.

"What are you doing up here invading my privacy?" It came out halfway between a reprimand and an expression of pleasure.

He smiled lazily, already fully dressed in his working gear, which suited him marvellously. Bush shirt, jaunty bright blue bandana carelessly knotted around his throat, fitted jeans, high boots. The only thing missing was the cool black akubra. "I have a right, don't you think?" he countered mildly. "I do own the place."

"I wasn't expecting you right outside my bedroom door." She was suddenly as nervous as a kitten. Should she rush inside and collect her matching satin robe?

"I figured it was all right, now it's morning." He answered with a touch of sarcasm.

"You didn't really think we were going to sleep together?" She held his gleaming gaze in case it fell to the telltale quick rise and fall of her breasts.

"Then you'd better not lead me into temptation," he warned. "What was that exciting little dance you did last night?"

"And didn't you love it!" she softly mocked, lifting her chin and spreading her hands in an exaggerated flamenco pose. "It started out as an ode to the rain god. I presume there is one around here?"

"Very much so," he confirmed, looking so sexy she thought his whole aura would engulf her. "Apparently your dance was so good he thought he'd reward you. Only one downpour, but you'll be surprised what a difference it'll make."

"So I'll have to do more dancing," she said, aware of the sudden acceleration of her pulses.

"I don't know if my heart can take it."

"Mine, either. Listen, do you mind if I get my robe?"

He continued to walk towards her taking in that beautiful body encased in satin. "When you look absolutely luscious as you are." His amber eyes were so brilliant they momentarily blinded her to her surroundings.

"I'll be back in a moment," she promised.

"Hurry. Because I want to have breakfast with you. Tell me, do you ride?"

She paused in the act of shouldering into her peach satin robe. "As in trains, buses?"

"As on horses."

She stepped back onto the verandah, tying the braided, silken cord. "Could I fake it?"

"No. Absolutely no. So you don't ride?"

"Why so scathing?" she said defensively. "I thought I was here to handle the Christmas functions. Which reminds me, I'm going to order the biggest tree I can get. It has to be synthetic. Spruce or something. As long as it's big. Is that okay? I'll arrange to have it flown in."

"From the sound of your voice I'm meant to acquiesce."

She curled her lovely mouth into a smile. "Does that mean yes?"

He nodded his head, a mass of deep sun-streaked amber waves, grown a little long on the nape. "When my mother was alive we had a tree. After she was killed everything stopped. All the fun. All the laughter. The only laughs I got were at boarding school and later at university."

"Well, don't feel down. We're going to have a wonderful Christmas tree this year. I know the exact place for it."

"So you've said. Where?"

"As it turns out we have to shift something," she said.

"What?" He turned directly to face her, his expression rather tense.

"The library table," she said. "Don't worry, it's going back."

"Why not put it to one side of the entrance hall?"

"No, no, you have to indulge me in this," she said. "Dead centre is perfect. That's the most commanding position and we can all see it in the round. Besides, the entrance hall is huge. Guests will be able to move around the tree easily providing they don't go mad and crowd it."

"My mother used to have it there," he said, his gaze moving away from her to the horizon.

"Then that's lovely, isn't it?" Angel said gently, thinking the spirit of Roxanne could be helping her.

Jake moved towards her with his silent, big-cat tread. "Why is it I want to kiss you every time I lay eyes on you?"

"Could it be because you're falling in love with me?" she asked, full of hope, while wonderful sensations began their glide all over her skin.

"Haven't you got enough men in love with you?" He wanted to touch her urgently.

"They're in love with my cooking."

"Though very good I'm sure it's the least of your charms." He surrendered to that driving impulse. He dipped his head, very gently, but so tantalisingly covering the full sensuous curves of her mouth with his own. "Could you really love me, mixed-up mortal man?"

How could she answer when her knees were buckling?

It was ages before either of them could come up for air. Both of them were in very deep.

"I could pick you up and carry you back into the bedroom," he told her huskily, the very thought making his head swim. "You're not a virgin."

"For heaven's sake, I'm twenty-five. How many lovers have you had?" She turned it back on him.

"Collectively?" He nipped her lips gently with his beautiful white teeth.

"The family friend Dinah Campbell, I'm sure. You're a bit casual about her. Isn't she flying in Friday?"

"Hell, is she?" He released her abruptly.

"Surely you knew?" she asked in amazement. "Didn't Gilly tell you? Don't you want her to come?"

"Questions, questions," he moaned. "Dinah's coming over for one thing, I'm sure."

"She's lonely when she's not in your bed?"

His shoulders moved impatiently. "Would you believe she's never been in my bed?"

"Noooo."

"It might be every girl's dream, but not in my bedroom," he scoffed. "When I have had an affair, it's been elsewhere. No, Angelica, Dinah is coming over to check you out. She wanted to handle all the functions, you know "

"I guessed as much." Angelica arched her beautifully marked black brows. "Is she up to the job?"

"Probably," he mused, stroking his clean-cut chin.

"Then why bother with me?" She put him on the spot.

"Isobel recommended you and you charmed me when you rang."

"Of course you had no idea who I was then."

"No, I found out too late." He dredged that up, not even knowing why.

It had quite an effect on Angelica. She turned on her heel. "What a rotten thing to say. You really are a bastard."

He laughed, despite himself. "So I am. I'm sorry."

"No you're not sorry," she said sternly. "You'll say something like that again, because you're so judgmental."

"And there's the rub. I'm not usually," he said, following her into the bedroom. "It has something to do with you, my angel."

"Amoral old me." She sailed into the dressing room and began pulling out clothes. "You've got to put a stop to this, Jonathon."

He had almost made it to the door, thinking he had better leave, now he snaked out a long arm, grasping her around the waist. "Show me how."

"You want me to get in touch with your cousin first. I was the victim then. I don't want to be now."

"Sure," he sighed. "But why did Carly believe you had an affair with her husband?" Through the thrum of conflict, he was aware of the tremendous intimacy that was building up between them. He could feel her trembling. He could feel her magical body through the shining satin. She was taking him places where he had never been before. Inciting emotions that made him say contrary things to her.

Her voice was torn. "This is unbearable." She made a half-hearted movement to get away from him. "Your cousin couldn't have named me at all. Why don't you speak to her, you're such a doubting Thomas? Then, maybe, we can start all over again." She stared briefly into his eyes. Found them strangely troubled. "You'd better go now." Before this tiny scuffle tipped into something else.

"I don't think I can move from this spot."

She turned her head away, feeling close to tears. "What do you want of me, Jonathon? We scarcely know one another yet here we are—"

"Desperate to fall back on that bed," he completed her thought, his voice quiet and contemplative. "It can't be all that unusual to want a woman on sight."

"You must go," she said. "Really."

He grasped a handful of her hair and tilted up her head. "Why don't I just lock the door?"

She shook her head. "Because you think I'm a bad girl."

"No. Maybe I'm afraid of you. Of what you could do to me." He began shaking out her sleep-tousled hair. It was like skeins of heavy silk.

"Talk to me, Jonathon." She found herself winding her arms around him, almost protectively. "How could you be afraid of me? Why?"

"God knows! Feelings," he said, resting his chin on her head. "So much so soon it's like an avalanche. I didn't even know you, yet I hated seeing Huntley's hand on you. Hated him. My reaction was so excessive I veered away from remembering. Yet you stayed with me only to be brought forth in my dreams."

"As I remembered you," she confided, looking back over the intervening three years.

There was such a sweetness, an understanding to her tone he found himself continuing the moments of self exploration. "It's that loathing of Huntley, my disgust at his callous hand that makes me say harsh things," he said, shadows gathering on his golden-bronze face. "My father had the cruellest tongue and a way of glaring. I guess I worry there's more than a bit of him in me after all."

"You're not cruel, Jonathon," she said, shaking her head, imagining him as a defenceless child taking that kind of treatment from a formidable father.

"God, I hope not!" His voice carried the sounds of his deepest concerns. "You have that healing touch. It's true, isn't it, Angel?" He looked down, his gaze irresistibly zooming in on her mouth, a natural tender red like crushed strawberries. He couldn't look at it without putting his own mouth to it, covering the plush, receptive surface.

A moment of sliding back into a dream world, then he put her away from him. "You're right, I shouldn't be here. I should be doing my job. I have a station to run. But first, I want you to have breakfast with me."

"I'll get breakfast for you, you mean," she told him eagerly, swinging about to spy out her clothes. "I promise you you'll lick the plate clean."

He laughed and walked to the door, moved by her soft, lovely mood. "In return I'll find the time to teach you to ride," he promised, and sketched a brief salute. "Ten minutes. No more."

She waved him away, suddenly incredibly happy. "I'm aiming for five."

The rest of the day passed very swiftly. There was much to be done. In Clary she had a fine, capable, enthusiastic lieutenant ready to do everything to make these Christmas celebrations work. Even Stacy and Gillian got into the spirit of it. It was clear they found her quite unthreatening, indeed they all did quite a lot of laughing as Angelica took them through her plans for the various functions one by one. "I think I might like Leah in on this," Angelica announced at one point. "If you all agree she's gifted—and she certainly is if you consider the sheer professionalism of that dress— she'll be able to help out with the decoration."

"But Mum and I want to decorate the tree, Angelica." Gilly looked dismayed. "We'd love to get involved."

"But of course. It's your home, Gilly. I'm only here as co-ordinator and supervisor. I'm talking about the Great Hall for Leah."

"Oh, that's all right then." Gilly looked relieved. "As

long as we don't have dear Dinah getting into the act. Mum and I aren't keen on Dinah.'' Her pretty mouth thinned.

"We should be able to avoid that," Angelica said hopefully. "I've spoken to Jake about the tree. We're going to shift the library table so it can soar dead centre."

"Shift the library table!" Stacy echoed, as though that was absolutely the worst thing that could happen. "But the library table has always been there, dear."

"Then it's time we shifted it. For the occasion anyway," Angelica coaxed. "Trust me, Stacy. It will look wonderful there."

"Yes, Mum, let Angelica handle it." Gilly joined forces. She let her blue eyes rest on Angel's tall, striking figure. Everything about her was perfect, she thought. Even her height, though she wouldn't want to be so tall herself. Angelica was wearing a simple pink top, but in a very nice sort of slinky fabric, teamed with a full pink skirt printed with huge cyclamen peonies. Not a dress-up outfit but it looked great. "I bet you brought some beautiful dresses with you," Gillian said wistfully. "If you had a moment I'd love you to take a look at what I'll be wearing. Compared to you it's all out of date. Mum and I haven't bought a thing since the last time we went shopping in Sydney. That was eighteen months ago." She groaned and let her head fall forward on the table.

"Your clothes are lovely, Gilly darling," Stacy remonstrated as if Gillian didn't fully appreciate how fortunate she was.

"No they're not, Mum. You're way behind the times." Gillian tugged rebelliously at her shirt.

"I'm sure Angelica can give you some guidance, pet." Clary patted Gillian's arm. "Why when you're all dolled up you look lovely. You too, ma'am." She nodded at Stacy. "If I was you two, I'd really go to town for the parties. Give everyone a surprise."

"But you're coming, too, Clary," Angel said. She didn't want Clary left out.

"I'm tempted to." Clary's cheeks went hot and ruddy with surprise.

"But of course you must!" Stacy's face lit up as though she'd only that minute thought of it. "You've been an absolute rock."

"That I have!" Clary nodded her agreement, not one to hide her light behind a bushel.

"Well, that's settled." Angelica looked around with satisfaction. "We might arrange a private dressing-up, but it has to be soon just in case we decide on something completely different."

"How? Isn't it all too late?" Gillian looked like she mistrusted her hearing.

"Never too late," Angel assured her blithely. "I have friends all over, including designers and boutique owners. Clever people who know how to dress their clients. All you need is the money."

"We have it if we need it," Stacy offered, pretty much like a schoolgirl. "Jake handles all the money. We can get it from him."

To Angelica, the modern working woman, that was quite bizarre. It seemed Victorian in fact. She turned to Clary for a little relief. "So you'll speak to Leah when she comes in?" Clary rolled up her sleeves.

"Better yet I'll get her up to the house and you can speak to her."

"Lovely."

Angelica was in Jake's study, sending off a batch of e-mails to various distributors when Leah, wearing another one of her enchanting hand-painted dresses, tapped gently on the door.

"You wanted to see me, Miss?"

Angelica clicked the e-mail away and looked up to smile. "Yes, Leah. Come in and take a seat. Mr. McCord has very kindly allowed me to use his study." She broke off as she realised Leah wasn't alone. Almost hidden behind her mother's skirt was one of the most adorable little girls Angelica had ever seen. She had a wonderfully engaging face and the huge melting black eyes of her mother, but her skin was a shade or two lighter and she had a head full of stunning toffee-coloured curls.

"You must be Kylee," Angelica said, delighted by the child. "How are you?"

The little girl grinned shyly but didn't speak, bunching her mother's skirt with her hand.

Leah gave her a little prod as though the child's silence might give offence. "Say hello to Miss."

Angelica heard the anxiety, felt a pang of pity. "That's all right, Leah," she said easily, thinking life for Leah must have been a grim business.

"She's shy."

"Hello, Miss," the child, knowing she was being talked about, piped up. Her bright expression turned earnest.

"It's lovely to meet you, Kylee. Come take a seat beside Mummy. We need to talk about all the Christmas parties we're going to have."

"With presents?" The very idea gave Kylee a huge buzz. She made a sudden rush for a chair and in the process took a tumble on the slightly raised edge of the Persian rug.

"Silly girl!" Anxiously Leah scooped her daughter up and deposited her rather hard into the leather chair. "I'm sorry, Miss," she apologised as though Angel was about to remonstrate. "I shouldn't have brought her."

"Whyever not? I love children. I'm a proud aunt already. My brother, Bruno, has a little boy just turned two. I'm godmother to two others. The children of girlfriends. Relax, Leah, everything is fine. What I want is to enlist your help with the decoration of the Great Hall. It will be in use for the Polo Ball. You're a creative person. You might be able to come up with some ideas? I believe in consulting clever people."

"Me, Miss?" Leah looked astounded.

"Yes, you, Leah." Angelica laughed. "Is that totally un-

expected? Please call me Angelica, or Angie, if you like.''
She looked steadily into the young woman's eyes.

"Better not, Miss,'' Leah said simply. "No one has ever
asked me to do anything before.''

"Well this is your big chance.'' Angelica leaned forward
encouragingly.

"Are children coming?'' Kylee chirruped.

"I told you you must be quiet, Kylee,'' her mother warned
in a quick aside.

"All you children are coming to the staff barbecue,''
Angelica told the child kindly, trying to see beyond Leah's
uptight manner to what experiences lay behind it. "And there
will be presents.''

Immediately Kylee started to bounce up and down in her
chair when oddly her mother seemed distressed.

"Why, Leah, whatever's wrong?'' Angelica asked in quick
concern.

"No one likes me. Or her.'' Leah dashed a hand across
her cheek.

"That can't be right.'' Angelica curled her fingers tightly
around her pen, almost as if she were going into battle.

"That's the way it is, Miss.'' Leah's long curly black
lashes languished on her cheeks. "I want everyone to like
me but they don't. The station ladies, they don't like me.
They don't want Kylee to play with their kids.''

"Have you any idea why?'' Angelica was amazed.

"Oh, different things,'' Leah said vaguely. "I can't talk
to people like I want. I can't say, hello Mick, hello Vince. I
tell you, them women are funny. They think I want to take
their man away. 'Course I don't. I learned men are cruel. Me
own man left me. Took off whoosh, just like that the minute
he knew I was pregnant. Reckoned it wasn't his. Reckoned
it could have been anybody's. It was his all right. He knew.''

"Life has been hard for you, Leah,'' Angelica said, seeing
that Leah needed lots of loving care let alone repair. "Where
did you get that scar?'' It was the first time Angelica had
seen it. Leah wore her shoulder-length dark hair side parted

and falling forward onto her cheeks. Now as she spoke she pushed the heavier side behind her ear, revealing a long welt of a scar running from temple to ear.

"The old man." Leah winced, putting her fingers to it. "Ran at me with a bottle," she said with droll disdain. "Drunk. Saturday night. Wasn't good to me. Reckon I'd be dead only Mr. McCord found out about me and Kylee and offered me a job at the homestead helpin' out. I'll never be able to thank him, but I try. I like it here at the house. Clary is kind to me. And my little one." She pointed a finger at Kylee who tried to grab it.

"But of course." Looking at Leah with her delicate exotic looks, a by-product of her mixed blood, Angelica could well see why some of the station wives might be wary of the effect of those looks on their menfolk. At the same time she felt Leah in her vulnerability of body and mind was seeing antipathy where there was none. She thought she might call a meeting of the station wives, citing plans for the staff barbecue as the reason. It would present an opportunity to find out why Leah should consider herself and her child outsiders. There were always two sides to a story.

Almost without thinking Angel hunted up a small notepad and a pencil and held it out across the table. "Would you like to draw like Mummy, Kylee?" she suggested to keep the child entertained.

Without a second's hesitation Kylee scrambled out of the chair and dashed around the desk. "Is this mine?" She grabbed the pad and pencil.

"If you want it to be." Angelica didn't think the station would miss a small notepad and pencil.

Kylee jumped back and laughed merrily. "I like you, Miss. You're nice. Other ladies tell me to be still when I can't be still."

"What other ladies?" Angelica looked to Leah.

"The Missus and Miss Gillian don't like Kylee running around the house." Leah squeezed her elegant fingers together. "She gets away from me sometimes when I work. She's a real little monkey."

Moments later four-and-a-half-year-old Kylee jumped up and presented Angel with her finished oeuvre.

"Goodness me!" Angel held the drawing in her hands, amazed at how easily and swiftly the child had done it. It wasn't the typical simple four-year-old drawing. It was of a tree. A quite extraordinary tree with thick gnarled branches and prop roots rising out of swift impressions of rocks and tufts of grass. "Kylee, this is very good," she said, much surprised. "I like it very, very much. Aren't you a clever girl." Clearly, Kylee, like her mother, had a gift.

"She knows her alphabet. She can count. She can spell lots of words," Leah said proudly. "Better than me. The nuns could teach me how to sew but they couldn't teach me anything else. I never saw much of the classroom. I had to help a lot with me foster mum."

"Were you happy there?" Angel had grave misgivings about the foster mum.

"I hated her," Leah said. "And him. Especially him."

Angelica very nearly moaned, thanking God for her parents and her happy childhood. "Well you've produced a very talented little girl." She tried to console. "This drawing I'm sure is far beyond her age ability. It looks like a real tree."

"It is." Leah gave Angel a kind of challenging look as though a white woman, however nice, couldn't possibly know. "This tree has great power. Kylee and me often go there to talk to it. It's one of the old spirits."

"It actually looks like one," Angelica said. "I'm going to keep this, Kylee," she told the child gently, "and I'm going to find you some drawing books and coloured pens and pencils. Would you like that?"

"To take home?" Kylee asked, her eyes huge.

"Where is home?" Angelica turned in the swivel chair to ask Leah.

Leah gave a radiant smile. "Mr. McCord give us a nice

bungalow. Best place I ever lived in in me life. I can show you if you like.''

"Yes I do like, Leah." Angelica leaned back in the deep comfortable desk chair. "I just can't quite figure out how I'm going to do it, but I'd like to help you. We can arrange a time for me to see your dress designs and your paintings. Charles Middleton told me he's bought a few off you and they're very good. I'm sure Charles would know.''

"And who might Charles Middleton be?" Leah giggled.

"Why, Charlie, the jackeroo."

"Oh, Charlie!" Leah rolled her eyes. "He's nice. He's funny. He's never been mean to me.''

"I should think not," Angelica said. "Charlie is a gentleman. You'll have to tell me who is mean to you, Leah. We'll take it up with Mr. McCord. For now I want to tell you my idea for a theme for the Polo Ball. I was going to get someone in, though I fancy I've left it a bit late, but maybe you could handle what I have in mind. With your aboriginal blood you'd have great affinity with the land, this extraordinary channel country. I'm thinking of a mural. A kind of dream landscape. Dreamtime, if you like. Sun, rocks, billabongs, waterlilies, all those marvellous birds, the vivid coloration that comes as such a shock. On the ceiling, and perhaps a little down the walls, depending on how you feel and how it turns out.''

Leah almost jumped out of her chair. "On the ceiling? You mean, like Michelangelo?" she asked with a great flare of interest. "The Sistine Chapel in Rome?"

"You know all about it?" Okay, Angelica thought, I'm surprised.

Leah smiled, looking happy and in the process quite beautiful. "I love looking at books about painting and artists. Only books I like. That would be a wonderful idea, but I'd have to do it all the time so I couldn't work here. I'd have to have ladders and trestles and everything.'' She threw out her arms as if to say this venture was on the level of building a city bridge.

"We'd better get cracking then," Angelica said. "I want other things to figure in that landscape, Leah. It's a polo theme. Would it be pushing it to ask if you can draw animals."

"'Course I can draw animals," Leah lightly scoffed. "What kind of animals? It's not gunna be kangaroos?"

"Horses." Angel sat back. "Polo ponies, to be specific, though they only call them ponies."

"Even Kylee can draw a horse."

"I can't," Angel freely admitted. "Can't ride one, either."

"No big deal, Miss." Leah smiled.

"So, a landscape, horses, floating umbrellas. The kind of striped umbrellas you see at polo matches."

"Never been to one," Leah said laconically.

"Never mind. I'll get you a brolly to copy. Sporting cups. There are dozens of them just behind you. Somehow Mr. McCord managed to acquire them. You can't back out now, Leah."

"I don't want to back out. That's great!" said Leah, nearly leaping out of her skin with excitement.

"Brilliant!" Angelica added for good measure, pleased at Leah's reaction. "My own idea of the ceiling in the hall is a featureless plain. You can shape it any way you like but let it reflect the station."

"I reckon we might get many flowers after the storm. I reckon last night was magic. It shoulda come to nothin'. I'd nearly forgotten what the rain tastes like, all clean and wet. Anyway I can draw flowers easy, the blue, blue sky, big rain bubbles like balloons. Maybe a couple of little kids sittin' under a tree. Doesn't have to be real?"

"Put your own stamp on it, Leah," Angelica said.

By six o'clock the following morning Angelica was down at the stables for her first riding lesson. If it was any help, she thought she was fairly brave, but she knew horses were temperamental as well as majestic creatures. If it came to a battle between her and any horse the horse would easily win. She guessed the secret had to be gentleness and sensitivity. She hoped she might be good at that.

When she arrived, right on time, Jake was already waiting for her. "Sleep in?" The amber eyes swept over her, taking in her appearance. She wore a short-sleeved blue cotton shirt tucked into tight-fitting designer jeans and a fancy silver and turquoise belt. On her head she wore a navy and white baseball cap turned the wrong way, and her thick hair was tied back in a plait.

She glanced at her watch. "Right on time, McCord."

"You're very cheeky, aren't you, for someone just about to have her first riding lesson?"

"I trust you with my life." She smiled, wondering how it was possible she had developed an enormous attachment to him virtually overnight. Maybe it was all the time she had dreamed of him. The years she had waited to see his unforgettable face in a crowd. An unforgettable face.

"I love the way you say that," he said, making a move toward her that caused a mad rush of pleasure. But then an aboriginal boy around sixteen emerged from one of the buildings in the huge stable complex, leading a bright chestnut horse.

"Here I am, boss." The boy laughed as though he and the horse had to be flagged down.

"Thanks, Benny." Jake, too, laughed as though at some private joke, then turned to give Angelica a faintly mocking look. "Say hello to your mount for the day. Her name's Ariel. And this grinning character is Benny. I only keep him on because he's very good with the horses."

"And I'm great muckin' out." Benny squinted up at Jake through the golden sunlight.

"Hello, Benny." Angelica smiled.

"Pleased to meet yuh, ma'am." Benny bobbed his curly dark head. "Yuh doin' pretty good to get the boss to teach yuh," he offered cheekily.

"The question is why?" Angelica asked.

"I'm curious to know if you're going to be your usual confident self or you're going to get jittery."

Benny smothered a laugh. "Thank you, Benny," Jake said.

"I'll be back when you need me. Good luck, ma'am."

There was so much devilment in those black eyes Angel began to examine the mare more thoroughly, wondering if its real name mightn't be Psycho. "This couldn't possibly be a set-up?" she asked thoughtlessly.

He glanced at her, narrow-eyed, as well he might. "I wouldn't dream of doing anything foolish, let alone potentially dangerous."

"God no! I'm so sorry. I spoke without thinking. Just tell me what I'm supposed to do."

"You might look and listen." He eased off. "As you can imagine the ideal is to be put on a horse before you can even walk."

"Which, of course, happened to you."

He turned to gaze at her, looking every inch the imperious male, determined not to surrender to her charm. "I don't know that I've actually met a woman who so enjoyed taking the mickey out of me."

She shrugged, trying not to laugh. "I'm not going to apologise. Especially when you can be very, very lordly. Anyway, you know what I mean."

"Yes, I do know what you mean, Miss De Campo, but then, you're outrageous."

"So you keep saying, but it feels good with you. For the rest of the lesson I promise to be on my best behaviour."

"Thank you for that. I'd hate to see you when you're behaving badly."

"Surely you don't want this to lead to an argument?" she coaxed, aware even at this hour of the morning the chemical attraction between them was highly explosive.

"The truth is I want to kiss you madly," he said with a touch of self-derision, "but we'll run overtime. Are you going to pay attention?"

She groaned with wry humour. "That's what I want to do because when you get to know me better you'll find I'm a very sweet woman."

He laughed shortly. "I'd prefer if you were—"

"What?" She threw up her dimpled chin. "Go on, Jonathon. I challenge you to tell me what you want me to be?"

"Try being this!" With one arm he reached for her, pulling her to him.

His skin was gold, his eyes were gold and his gaze intense. Heart pounding, she waited for his kiss, the world around them reduced to the power of two. His handsome face taut with emotional pressure, he lowered his head, kissing her so passionately, so possessively, her whole body gave one long rapturous convulsive shudder.

"Jonathon," she murmured when the world slowly stopped spinning, "don't do this to me if you don't mean it."

"Mean it?" He steadied his voice with an effort. "You want it. I want it. It's almost as though we have no say in the matter. At least it keeps you quiet for a time." He allowed himself the luxury of holding her beautiful body close.

He stopped her with one brief hard kiss, and then he looked around as though he'd just remembered where they were. The mare stood quietly, well schooled around humans. "My mother taught me to ride," he volunteered.

"You don't hate horses because of what happened to her?" Angelica asked very gently.

"That happened to my father. Not to me. For me riding and horsemanship has been one of life's greatest pleasures. My mother was a wonderful rider. Before she married—for years when she was a girl—she won many competitions for show jumping. That's why it was such a terrible irony she was killed in a riding accident."

"Were you there?"

He stared off across the cobbled courtyard. "I was there afterwards when they brought her in."

"I'm sorry." Sympathy gripped her. "This must still upset you."

"God, yes!" He sighed deeply. "I'll never forget it to my dying day. Her horse was a glorious animal. Habibah. My father shot it right in front of me. My mother would never have wanted that. It was a terrible accident. It could happen to any one of us."

"He was out of his mind with grief." Her beautiful eyes reflected his grief.

"Yes, but I always thought it was cruel and it made him cruel. It was as if another being took him over. There was no life for Stacy. Little enough for Gillian. It's obvious I look like my mother, but that was no comfort to him."

"But your father didn't crush you or your spirit."

He shook his head, his expression grim. "No matter how hard he tried. Why are we discussing this, Angelica?" He stared into her eyes. "We shouldn't be when I'm supposed to be giving you your first riding lesson. It's all about being calm around horses. Not tense."

"I'm a fatalist," Angelica said. "I believe what's to be will be."

He took hold of her shoulders firmly. "Then it appears to be destiny we were fated to meet again. You're a woman who can cause extreme emotions. The agony and the ecstasy."

"I'm afraid that's what love is," she pointed out quietly.

"Who's talking love?" he questioned, looking deeply into her eyes.

"A man can't grieve over what he doesn't love."

"No."

"Are you afraid loving might test you too much?"

"Surely it invites terrible vulnerability? A loss of autonomy. Losing the woman one loves can shatter a man's life forever. I'm not afraid of making a commitment, Angelica. I am afraid of falling in love with the wrong woman. A career-oriented woman, maybe, who'll go off and leave me. I'm pretty much stuck here. Coori is my life."

"Hey, tell me something I don't know," she tried to tease, though her heart contracted.

"Do you want to hear now or save it for after the lesson?" he asked laconically. "Poor old Ariel is being very patient."

"Of course she is!" Chastened, Angelica reached out an impulsive hand to stroke the mare's neck just as he'd been doing for much of the time they'd been talking, but the horse tossed its head and took a few steps back. "Already I've done something wrong," she said in dismay.

"Don't worry." His voice couldn't have been more gentle. "You moved a bit too quickly, that's all. Put your hand out and let her get your scent."

This time Angelica took her time and was rewarded when the mare lowered her muzzle into her palm, tickling it with its whiskers and snuffling contentedly. "Isn't she pretty?"

"Aren't you pretty," he said dryly. "You remind me of a high-stepping filly, as Ariel was not all that long ago. I take it you've never sat on a horse?"

She shook her head. "Never. I didn't even have a rocking horse when I was a child. Probably even as a four-year-old my legs would have touched the ground."

"Well they won't now. There's an art to all this, Angel. If you really want to ride and enjoy it you'll have to make an intelligent attempt to master the correct techniques. I'm going to tell you all about what we call the aids, the means of communicating with the horse. Legs, seat, hands, voice. It's all about learning to feel what the horse is doing beneath you and influencing those movements. You'll appreciate it's the legs that create the power—I assume you've been to the races?"

"Not only that, I've won Fashions on the Field twice. Though I was runner up first time."

"What else? You regularly back outsiders that come in at a hundred to one?"

"I'd love to tell you that. The fact is I always lose. So the legs move the horse. The rider's hands guide it hopefully in the right direction?"

"Is there anything I can tell you?"

"Yes. Are you going to allow me to get into the saddle?"

"If you think you can keep your balance. You have to sit securely and centrally."

"I can do that," she stated confidently. "This is going to be exciting."

"Not on poor old Ariel it isn't. She's a quiet, sweet-tempered, well-schooled horse. You're such a tearaway I'd hate to put you on anything else. Your voice will be a big asset. It's a voice even a horse would stop and listen to. Your voice tells the horse whether you're pleased with it or not. An extrovert person such as yourself—"

"Thank you—"

"—can coax a little more out of a quiet horse. I wouldn't put an excitable person, for instance, on an equally excitable horse."

Challenge glowed in her dark eyes. "You're saying I'm excitable?"

"You are when you and I get together."

She couldn't dispute that. "It sounds fine—doesn't it?— fatal attraction, but it's scary."

"Especially when my dreams throw up all sorts of scenarios," he admitted, releasing his breath slowly.

"You dream about me?" She was thrilled and astonished.

It would be so simple to deny it, but he didn't. It was a step forward for him. "When a man slaves all day, his dreams tend to take off. I've dreamt about you, Angel. I've even gone so far as to—"

"Don't tell me." She flushed.

He stood there in the streaming sunlight looking very handsome, male and mocking. "All right, I'll let you find out. Now do you want to mount this horse or don't you?"

She gave her long thick plait an absent flick. "Of course I do. You're the one doing the flirting."

"Flirting?" He raised a bronze brow.

"Haven't you heard the word before? I'm not complaining, mind you. I like it."

"Then you think you know what you're doing?"

"Not really," she confessed, "but I'm no wimp."

"Hell no! You're full of spirit. If I gave you a leg up do you think you could swing the other over Ariel's back? Alternatively we could mount from the fence."

"Listen, I'm an athlete. One fit, long-legged lady." She was ready to rise to the challenge.

Moments later she was sitting triumphantly in the saddle, back straight, shoulders square, no suspicion of a slump.

"That was damned good!" he exclaimed in admiration, looking up at her with approval. She was seated comfortably and balanced. It seemed she was a natural.

"Why sound so surprised?" She looked down into his remarkable eyes.

His gaze narrowed and darkened. "I know so little about you, but that, I guess, is all part of the excitement. Teaching you, Angel, is going to be a breeze."

Which was exactly how it turned out.

CHAPTER SEVEN

DUSK was drawing near. Jake halted in the shade of one of the coolabahs lining a shallow gully to sweep off his akubra. God, that felt good! The cooling breeze ruffled through his sweat-soaked head, bringing some relief. He couldn't wait to have a long relaxing shower and wash his red-sand-grimed hair. It had been another day of stifling heat yet the sloping grasslands had sprouted tiny purple flowers that rode the tips of the soft cane grass in wave after wave. That was the result of one good downpour courtesy Angel's exotic rain dance. The inflammatory flamenco encore had been entirely for him and that had brought equally tumultuous results!

The air around him was deliciously scented with wild passion fruit flower. He breathed in deeply, worshipful of this great ancient land. Though the heavy purple passion fruit looked inviting and tasted good, aboriginals on the station refused to touch it. The fruit belonged to one of their spirit beings who didn't take kindly to having it stolen. Though such an idea half amused him, he rarely ate the fruit himself even when his throat was parched.

It was another remarkable sunset. Fiery-red clouds billowing on the horizon reminded him of atomic mushrooms. Now the sky was turning the colour of smoke shot through with lavender. Galahs above him chewed away contentedly on blossom and leaves, making quite a racket. His black gelding suddenly chose that moment to loudly neigh and the birds took off in a flock of pearl-grey and deep pink, shrieking in protest as they sped further down the quiet lagoon.

Everywhere in this land he loved was colour and movement. Life and death. Coori was a haven for wildlife. Even as he gazed up at the darkening vault of the sky a falcon

110

with its claws spread casually selected a bird from the flock. It curved away with its prey to its nest in the low eroded hills. Falcons never missed. Their speed of attack was amazing. He replaced his wide-brimmed hat and rode on, aware these days there was an urgency in getting home, a feeling of pleasure and heart-lifting excitement.

It was all due to the woman he now thought of as Angel, which just showed how much she was getting to him. She certainly had power. It was extraordinary how having her in the house had made everyone, not just him, come alive. He'd almost forgotten what happiness was like; all but forgotten how beautiful life could be. Sometimes it seemed it was all backbreaking work. Even when he was near exhausted there was the business side of the operation that demanded a lot of his time.

So that was his life. A lot of work. Little time for play and even less time to find himself a wife. This was the common plight of the man on the land, especially when the situation was exacerbated by the remoteness of a cattle station. His womenfolk, Stacy and Gillian, were fragile, he knew. That was the result of the hard loveless years under his father when life had almost been reduced to a daily battle. He would be very very different with his own children. That he vowed, even as he feared some terrible tragedy could unleash a latent ruthlessness in him. He was his father's son after all. He could hear his father's voice in his own tones. It was true, as Angel had intuited, he feared his own genes.

At twenty-eight he now felt a profound need for a family of his own. He supposed he might be in search of his lost childhood through the eyes of a little son. To have a child, he needed a woman. The right woman. A woman who was capable of being the stabilising centre of family life. In so many, many ways Angel was that woman. She had strength, she had humour and a sunny, positive nature. Combined with all the rest, God knows, all he could think of these days was getting her into his bed, though he knew it wasn't going to happen without the all important development of trust.

He wanted her and from her passionate responses he couldn't fail to know she wanted him, but they both knew he had called into question her dignity. Everything really depended on him. He'd known so much uncertainty in his life, his wariness, especially with profound attachments, wasn't going to disappear overnight. Most likely he was wrong about what he thought he had seen at Carly's party. Wasn't he the man endlessly pursuing perfection? In thrall to the unattainable? From a lonely small child the portrait of his mother had kept her alive for him. She remained perfect, a princess. In reality she was a stumbling block when he sought the one special woman to measure up.

Then his eyes fell on Angel, resulting in his having to turn a spotlight on himself and his own emotional difficulties.

At least she was working wonders for Stacy and Gillian. Both were opening out like daisies after a shower of rain. It was Angel who filled the house with laughter and sunshine. She took such joy in everything it had rubbed off on his family. Even Clary, who had given him the impression she was tired of it all and wanted to retire, had found a new lease on life. She'd told him she was having a ball being Angel's "right hand."

Angel had even looked further, giving support and attention to that much abused young woman Leah. She had all kinds of ideas for Leah and her child. He knew Leah was gifted. He had seen her paintings, but he hadn't known little Kylee had inherited her mother's talent. In his broad experience aboriginal people were natural artists anyway. They'd been decorating caves since time immemorial.

When he entered the house he was confronted by a great beautiful Christmas tree—God, it had to be at least fifteen feet—soaring into the double space of the entrance hall. Its green upper branches were decorated with glittering baubles: frosty white bells, red, green, gold and silver balls, little ornaments galore. Angel was up a ladder dressed in a red T-shirt and tight jeans, an outfit that made the most of her beautiful breasts, long legs and tall willowy figure. She was busy tying a silver-winged cupid to one of the pendulous branches. A shorter ladder was set up on the other side.

"Hi!" she called brightly, giving him a lovely welcoming smile. "It arrived."

"I can see that. You haven't wasted any time. Be careful up there."

"Want to join me?" It was without provocation, more like one big kid to another.

"I'd love to, but I have to take a shower first. I'm as grimy as they come."

"You look great!" He did. All the time. He was a fabulous-looking man who somehow managed to look incredibly glamorous in cowboy gear. It was a kind of beauty that belonged only to a man, Angelica thought, staring down. Heroic. Sometimes she thought it was a beauty impossible to equal. Amber curls clung to his head and his nape. His golden-bronze skin was sheened by sweat. The rest of him took a lot of beating. He was six-three of dynamic male and superbly fit.

"Damn it all, Angel, be careful," he called at a rush, as the ladder, not all that stable, rocked slightly. No doubt due to her prolonged staring at him.

"Well, if you will distract me."

"Why start at the top?" he asked, experiencing a nostalgia that was a combination of the remembered joy and grief he kept in his heart.

"I'm very methodical," she explained. "I start at the top and work down. Gilly is going to help me. She's gone off for another box of baubles. Aren't they gorgeous?"

"I bet they cost an arm and a leg?" He gave a mock shudder, moving closer to finger a green branch.

"Of course they did, but they're positively essential."

"I agree."

He directed a smile at her that was so much like a kiss Angelica had to lean against the ladder for support.

"What's this supposed to be?" he asked, still fingering the

synthetic branch. "I'm not big on trees from the Northern
Hemisphere, but I take it it's a spruce?"

"Good guess. It's supposed to be a balsam fir. I think the
difference is the cones on the fir point upwards like the can-
dles on a Christmas tree. On the spruce and other conifers
they hang down."

"We learn something every day." He was about to move
off when Leah, holding tightly to the hand of her little girl,
arrived from the direction of the kitchen. She came to a halt
when she saw Jake, giving him a sunny smile. "Evenin', Mr.
McCord."

"Hello, there, Leah," he responded in an easy friendly
fashion. "And how are you, Miss Kylee?" he asked, low-
ering his golden gaze to the child.

"I'm good," Kylee announced with a beaming smile, then
immediately blotted her copy book by breaking free of her
mother's restraint. She launched herself at Angelica sitting
up on the ladder. "Hi, Miss?" she called happily, looking
for all the world like she was about to climb up and join
Angelica. Instead, before anyone could divine her intention,
in the unpredictable way of children, she gave the ladder a
surprisingly good shake.

Her mother shrieked, watching in horror as Angelica
leaned forward in an effort to clutch the ladder's sides. It
only took half a second more before her right foot became
dislodged, sliding perilously out of the rung.

Please God, let me bounce, Angelica prayed on the way
down. This was no time for injury, big or small.

Jake moved with alacrity, positioning himself to get his
arms under her, staggering for a moment, as he struggled to
hold on to her before the power in his legs steadied him and
allowed him to maintain his balance.

"Gracious!" Angelica, no featherweight, wrapped her
arms gratefully around his neck. "Aren't you strong?"

"I'd turn into Hercules for you." He levered her higher,
feeling the familiar stirring of desire. She could always work
that particular miracle.

"I don't think Hercules could do better." She arched back languorously, hair tumbling, both of them shocked out of the pleasure of the moment by the sound of Leah scolding little Kylee.

"What did you think you were doing, naughty girl?" she questioned, a reflection of the countless times she'd been asked that herself. But Kylee, used to the nervy, anxious side of her mother, scurried like a little mouse over to Jake, wrapping her arms around his long legs. "You naughty girl!" Leah fretted, making for Kylee, looking very much like she was going to smack her.

Angelica slid instantly to the ground, alerted to trouble, while Jake held up his hand.

"Stop, Leah. She's only four."

"Nearly five," Leah corrected, trying to pull out of her uptight state. "Why do I have a daughter like her? She's always getting into trouble."

"She's just a child," Jake reminded her. "You mustn't hit her, Leah. I won't allow it."

An odd kind of anger was rising from him, causing Angelica to run a soothing hand up and down his arm.

"There's no harm done," she said quickly, understanding Leah's vulnerable history. "It's anxiety that's making you cross, isn't it, Leah? You're always worried some bad thing will happen to you and Kylee?"

"I've had more'un my share of bad things," Leah responded bleakly, her expression momentarily full of the violence she'd experienced.

"That's all over now, Leah," Jake said, his tone softening.

"I hope so, Mr. McCord."

"You have my word."

He stood there every inch master of Coori station, Angelica thought. And a man of his word.

"While you're on Coori nothing bad will ever happen to you or Kylee, but you must promise me to be gentle with her. You experienced terrible things. All the more reason you can't let anything bad into Kylee's life."

Leah shook her head. "She's all I got. I love her."

"Of course you do," Jake said, knowing that was perfectly true; indeed Leah was trying very hard to make something of herself.

Still Angelica could feel he was disturbed. Very likely for reasons of his own.

"Did you want to see me, Leah?" she asked by way of diversion, feeling Kylee's sweet little hand slip into hers.

"Yes, Miss." Leah was glad of the change of subject. "It's about the Hall. I worked out lots of things I'm gunna do. I sketched it out on paper."

"Oh that's splendid!" Angel turned to Jake. "We have our ideas for the Great Hall. Leah as the artist in residence is going to do it." Or I hope she is. A sudden wave of doubt rose to her throat. His handsome face could look so formidable sometimes.

"Really? I assume you were going to consult me?"

"Of course." She stared at him, surprised but then not. She could see the way his lean body was braced. "I was waiting until we had something properly worked out."

"I can't tell you how relieved I am to know that," he said crisply. "Remember what I told you, Leah."

"Yes, sir," Leah answered.

"Okay, then. I'm off to take that shower. Be seeing you, Kylee." His expression smoothed out into his wonderful smile.

"See yuh. Mr. Jake," Kylee chirruped. "I jus' wanted Miss to come down," she explained. "Didn't want to make her fall."

"Of course you didn't." Angelica squeezed the child's hand. "You can stay and help with the decorations, if you like?" She looked to Jake to see if that was okay with him, but he was moving away.

"Jus' push her out, Miss, when you're ready," Leah said. "I gotta go. I got lots to think of if I'm gunna do the Hall."

"Let's see what you have in mind, Leah." Jake paused

long enough to say. "You said you had some sketches on paper?"

"Yes, sir. I'll bring 'em."

"Fine. I'm looking forward to seeing them. Who, by the way, is doing the flower arranging?" He glanced back at Angelica, his amber eyes sardonic.

Before she could formulate a fitting answer, he disappeared, all powerful lean elegance.

"Now you be a good girl, Kylee." Leah moved to cuddle her child who threw loving arms around her mother's neck.

It offered Angelica an opportunity to hurry after Jake, catching him at the end of the passageway.

"What did you get so angry about?" She swooped to clutch his arm.

"My dear Angelica, I'm not angry." He appeared to tower over her when he wasn't.

"Cross, then," she amended. "I hate to mention this when you're being so lordly, but you did give me carte blanche."

"Did I?" He pinned her with a stare.

"Oh, Jonathon, don't be like this." She put out an appealing hand. "Did my falling off the ladder shake you up?"

"You'll do anything to get attention," he drawled, unwilling in that moment to admit just how much.

"Are you worried Leah might mistreat Kylee?" She looked at him with understanding and concern.

"I can't totally discount it," he mused. "Violence breeds violence. I've seen it over and over again. I won't have anything happen to that child." A certain grimness settled on his striking features.

"I understand your fears, Jonathon." Angelica became aware she always used his name in their more emotional moments. "But I think in Leah's case, you could be overreacting."

"How much experience can you draw on?" he challenged. "Aren't you the young woman who had the ultimate happy childhood?"

"That doesn't mean I haven't seen a lot of unhappiness. I

have a close friend who found herself in a violent marriage. I could scarcely credit it even when I knew it was true. He's a doctor, believe it or not, from a highly respected family. He took an oath to keep people well. Kylee is a happy, bouncy, little girl. Leah is doing a good job of mothering. It's her ingrained anxieties that make her responses a little harsh. She's more bark than bite.''

"I recognise that, Angel," he said more reasonably, "just as I recognise the years of pent-up anger in her. I saw enough anger in my time. Anyway what's this about the Hall?" He shook his mood off.

"The Hall?"

"You're not losing your memory?"

"Excuse me, I was waiting until you were ready to listen. When you—"

"Cooled off?" he supplied wryly.

"Exactly." Unable to stop herself she leaned forward and kissed his cheek, her soft lips deliciously rasped by his faint beard. "You're a good man, Jonathon McCord," she said, "if a tad complicated."

"And you want a good man?"

"You could very well be my last chance," she said teasingly.

"Then I now pronounce you my wife." He set his two hands to cup her face before dropping a kiss on her mouth.

"Is that a first, or do you do it all the time?" she asked when she was able.

"All right, the wedding's off."

"I thought it might be."

"Get ready to show me all this stuff with Leah," he called as he strode away.

"Would Sir like to see it before or after dinner?" she called with mock servility.

"Just so I see it," he said.

When she returned to the hall she found Gillian in the act of sending Leah and Kylee away. Leah looked upset and

Kylee's entrancing little face was all crinkled up as if she was about to burst into tears. Angelica caught her breath in dismay wondering why Gillian, who had so much, couldn't be kinder and act less the daughter of the manor.

"Oh, Gilly, I did ask Kylee to stay," she said in a coaxing voice. "Christmas is all about children, don't you think?"

Gillian stared back at her, going a little red. "I thought it would be nice just us two," she protested, a young woman starved of her father's affection and excessively attached to the people she liked as a result. She liked Angel. And she liked Charlie. "Surely Kylee should have her tea and go to bed." Kylee who was far from lacking in intelligence, began to sob while her mother's black eyes flashed indignantly.

"A little longer won't matter and she's here now," Angelica pointed out as cheerfully as she could. "I did promise her."

"Very well," Gillian replied, with that odd tightening of the lips Angelica had noted before. Probably she had copied it from her father. It didn't look natural to her.

"I don't imagine she's seen so many pretty things in her whole life." Angelica smiled reassuringly at Kylee who had miraculously turned off her sobs to roll her huge liquid eyes.

"Neither have I," Gillian answered so shortly Leah backed away.

"I'll go home now, Miss." She addressed Angel. "I wanna go."

Kylee who appeared to have a decided mind of her own and, as Angelica had so recently pointed out to Jake, was not in the least cowed, pulled free of her mother. "Wanna stay."

"As you wish, Leah." Angelica caught the little girl firmly by the hand. "Kylee can wait with us for a while. Okay, Gilly?" She turned to face the younger woman.

"She's welcome," Gillian managed to her credit, although she was still flushed.

"Don't forget Mr. McCord wants to see what we've planned, Leah," Angelica reminded the young aboriginal woman. "If you wouldn't mind coming back in an hour?"

"What have you planned?" Gillian asked, in a high, surprised voice, spinning around to stare at Leah.

"You'll see." Angelica promised. "It's a design for a mural. It's to go on the ceiling of the Great Hall. That's if it all comes together."

"And Leah is going to do it?" Gillian's pretty blue eyes registered amazement.

"Yes she is," Angelica confirmed, while Leah stared fixedly at the parqueted floor. "Leah is very artistic."

"I'm goin', Miss," Leah said, acutely aware of Gillian's surprise and apparent resentment. She turned, looking so vulnerable Angel felt her heart ache with pity.

"Why is she so upset?" Gillian asked, startled by Leah's flight.

"You were a little short with her, Gilly. I'll make sure she's all right." Angelica dashed after the tiny Leah, easily overtaking her before she reached the kitchen.

"Please Leah," she begged. "Gillian doesn't mean anything. She's not an unkind person. It's just that she thinks she has to act in a certain way."

Leah blinked and swallowed. "She's not going to make a friend of an aboriginal woman, you mean. It's better to keep out of the way."

"That's giving in, Leah. I know you're a fighter. You're going to become the person you were meant to be."

Leah's delicate head shot up. "Why am I hurtin'?" she asked with simple dignity. "Why am I always hurtin'?"

"Because you've been severely wounded," Angelica said. "You never feel certain how you're going to be treated. There are lots of good people in this world who are going to help you. Try not to look for threat where there isn't. Gilly doesn't dislike or look down on you. She recognises in her heart there's a lot to you. She just finds it easier to treat you like a servant. It's the way she was reared."

"But I am a servant," Leah pointed out very simply.

"You have talents to lift you into a different league. Talents you're already calling on. Everyone needs a helping hand. I've had many people kind enough to help me, now I'm going to find a way to help you.''

"You'll go away."

That silenced Angelica, plunging a knife into her heart. Go away? Never see Jonathon again? It was not to be borne. "Well I'm here now," she said firmly. "It may be that you'll do very much better for yourself in the city where there's more scope for your special gifts. You do have them.''

"Yes." Leah lifted her head proudly.

"So prove it," Angelica said warmly, taking Leah's fine-boned hand. "You've had to be very tough to survive lots of bad situations. I've been hired to run these functions. I have to prove myself. So do you.''

Somehow that had the right effect. Leah grinned broadly. "Be back in an hour, Miss," she said.

Thirty minutes later Jake rounded the corridor into the entrance hall feeling much more relaxed and refreshed. "Hey, you've been working hard!" he called out in admiration, looking up at the Christmas tree.

The tree looked majestic dressed in lustrous bells and balls and sparkling ornaments with jewel-like glints of ruby and emerald, gold and silver.

"It's like a fairy tale, isn't it, Jake?" Gillian turned a happy, smiling face to her half brother. "Oh, I'm so looking forward to everything. It's so exciting and we're going to have tons of presents massed around the tree. Angelica has wonderful ideas for those carved nymphs on the stairs. We're going to dress up the stairway with velvet swags and painted pine cones and things.''

"That sounds great, Gilly," he told her gently, his gaze moving to beautiful sensual Angelica who was holding in her hands the Christmas angel dressed in a gossamer-like white-and-gold gown with golden wings and a golden halo on her amber curls.

"We're not finished yet." She smiled her pleasure. "We've got to have fairy lights. All white, I think. Some frosty snow in the desert. But we've elected you to place our angel on top. I thought the amber curls were a nice touch.''

"You selected it with me in mind?'' He stared at her with mocking golden eyes.

"I think she's exactly right in this house,'' Angelica pronounced.

"Okay now.'' He started towards her, hoping she'd planned on lots of mistletoe when a little voice carolled, "Wait for me!''

"Good heavens, Kylee, where did you come from?'' Jake laughed, much taken with this child as she scurried out of the shadowed passageway, gulping down cake.

"Been to the kitchen,'' she told him joyfully. "Clary gave me tea. Are yuh gunna put the Christmas angel up, Mr. Jake?''

"On second thought, you can help me.''

"Can I?'' Kylee squealed, her huge eyes flashing sparkling lights.

"I should be able to lift you without killing myself. Now Miss Angelica was a different story.''

"I thought you were interested in Herculean tests,'' Angelica reminded him, watching him lift the child like a bundle of feathers and carry her up the ladder.

Near the top, bracing himself securely, Jake reached out his long arm while Kylee placed hers over his as he set the angel into position. "There, done!'' he cried triumphantly.

"Done!'' Kylee threw back her toffee-coloured head and laughed then she leaned forward and gave Jake a smacking kiss on the cheek, her free hand stroking his face.

Angelica, watching this touching scene from beneath, found herself caught up by longing for a happy married life. A husband who was both lover and best friend. She also wanted children. She was twenty-five, nearing twenty-six. She couldn't help thinking she was moving further away from the optimum time to have children. And she wanted four. It was the dilemma facing many career women like her. Put off having children into the late thirties never mind the forties and risk not being able to conceive at all. The medical profession had aired their warnings.

Gillian grabbed her hand. "Would you believe that little kid kissing Jake?"

"I think it's lovely, don't you?" Angel's dark eyes were on man and child as they slowly descended the ladder.

"Yes, she's a cute little thing." Gillian gave a warm smile. "Wherever did she get those orange curls?"

"I guess we'll never know. Could be genetic, but surely there are aboriginal tribes in the Centre with blond and bronze hair?"

"Yes there are," Gillian recalled. "Leah is very attractive, isn't she, in her way?"

"Very," Angelica agreed. "It would be wonderful if she could find herself a good man this time. She and Kylee deserve a better life."

"She should thank Jake for rescuing her," Gillian said. "Not everyone cares, you know."

"Well I do," said Angelica with emphasis.

CHAPTER EIGHT

FROM the moment Dinah Campbell arrived Angelica could see why Stacy and Gillian found her an intimidating guest in their home. The forceful Dinah acted as if she were the owner of Coori with the McCord women brief tenants. Dinah Campbell wasn't one of the world's underdogs. She was supremely self-confident, and always looked everyone straight in the eye. Physically very attractive, she had genuine platinum-blond hair, which she wore in a short, sexy tousled crop, apple-green eyes, good lightly tanned skin, trim athletic body, and to cap it off she was a cool dresser. All in all she made a very eye-catching package.

But her manner! Miss Campbell appeared to attach much importance to herself as the only child of a landowning family with money to burn. Dinah herself already possessed more money than she actually needed from her maternal grandfather with the full expectation of in time gathering in the lot. The trouble was, wealth didn't always vouchsafe niceness of manners, Angelica thought, watching Dinah airkiss first her hostess then Gilly, making it seem they were honoured to have her pop in, before turning what used to be called a gimlet eye on Angel.

"So you're the caterer?" she asked for openers, managing to make it sound vaguely insulting.

"I see myself more as a Celebrity Organiser." Angelica smiled, determined not to take offence. "Angelica De Campo. How are you, Miss Campbell?"

"Oh fine, fine." Though Dinah's accent was well-educated, her voice timbre was not all that easy on the ear. "Good heavens, you must be all of six feet?" She directed her gaze to some point above Angelica's dark head as though clouds were billowing there.

Used as they were to Dinah's abrasive style, Stacy and Gillian looked at one another shell-shocked, but Angelica laughed it off.

"Yes," she said calmly. "All it takes is two inches of heel."

"I imagine it's a sore point?" Dinah's green eyes were so drilling she could have been trying to punch holes in Angelica's glowing, olive-skinned flesh.

"Not at all. I figure it means I can eat more," Angelica said tongue-in-cheek. They were all still standing on the verandah where they had grouped to greet the Outback aristocrat but now Angelica decided the only course open to her was to excuse herself.

"Lovely to meet you, Miss Campbell." She smiled, already on the move. Everyone told little white lies as a social lubricant. "I must see how Leah's getting on."

She couldn't have picked a better cue. "Leah? Really?" Dinah's artfully darkened eyebrows shot up to her shaggy fringe. "Isn't she the aboriginal girl with the child? Why would you have to see her?" It was clearly a demand that needed answering but even Angelica was at a loss as to a civil response. She looked to Stacy as mistress of Coori to say something, to put Miss Campbell in her place would be good—but Stacy's mouth opened and closed soundlessly. Plainly in Dinah's company she lost all confidence when confidence wasn't her thing.

Dinah was still waiting for an explanation, wearing a slightly frowning expression. After all, she had asked a question.

Well that's it, Angelica thought. Obviously she believes everything that happens on Coori is her business and her long friendship with Jake is going to end in only one way. With a spectacular Outback wedding. The joining of two dynasties. McCord-Campbell. Such-was-life Angelica had to ask herself if it mightn't be true, and she herself fitted into the Passing

Sexy Fling category. "Leah is being a great help to me," she offered finally, continuing to sound pleasant and calm.

"Please come back for lunch," Stacy called after her, looking nerve-racked.

"Will do." Angelica took off down the front steps before she threw caution to the winds, giving Stacy and Gillian a cheerful little wave. Both of them for their own good had to find their tongues.

Dinah meanwhile went to the balustrade, peering after Angelica's rapidly receding figure. She was intent on finding out which way Miss De Campo was heading. It appeared she was making for the Great Hall, which really begged another question.

"Well!" she said co-conspiratorially, turning back to the McCord women with raised brows. "She's a surprise."

"Who?" Stacy enquired, just to hold up the inevitable.

"Why, Miss De Campo. Who else?" Dinah shrugged.

"In what way?" This was awful. This was excruciating, Stacy thought. Couldn't Angelica have stayed? Stacy regarded Angelica as very brave.

"She's a little bit too sure of herself," Dinah said. "When one thinks about it, she's only here to do a job. She even swaggers."

"Crap!" Gillian, having picked up that crude expression from Charlie, decided to use it.

"Well I never!" Dinah looked at Gillian, near aghast. "That's very rude isn't it, Gilly?"

"I thought you were the one being rude." Gillian darted a desperate look towards her mother. "Angelica is a lovely person. She's very kind." And more than a match for you.

"Well she would be, wouldn't she?" Dinah lightly jeered. "As I said, she's here to do a job. A job, incidentally, I could have done with pleasure."

"But Jake couldn't have had enough confidence in you," Gillian said, going red. "I don't want to be unpleasant, Dinah, you're our guest. But I hope you're not going to start on Angelica because she's so beautiful."

Dinah pondered that almost derisively. "Beautiful?" Maybe to Gillian's standards was implied. "She's very striking sure, but, Gilly, and I'm sure this is your true opinion, she's way too tall. In fact she'd be very hard-pressed to find a man who didn't have to look up at her."

"Jake doesn't," Stacy offered with satisfaction, then immediately looked away to get back her strength.

But Dinah viewed Stacy's small neatly dressed figure as though Stacy had been attempting a little joke. "Jake doesn't have to look up to any woman," she offered complacently, "but knowing Jake as well as I do, I've only one thing to say. She's definitely not his cup of tea. And that bust! It's really too voluptuous."

"Well no one is ever going to say that about me as long as I live," Gillian, who was flat-chested, complained. "Busts are definitely big time."

Angelica found Leah and Kylee in the Great Hall. Kylee, seated at a little child-size desk, was happily trying to copy what her mother was doing while Leah was up on a trestle working on one side of her mural.

They both cried, "Hi!" as soon as Angelica walked in, their faces near identical in the contentment of expression. Leah had already solved the big problem of covering the background by having one of the maintenance men on the station allotted to her by Jake spray paint the ceiling and the back feature wall a beautiful dense blue like the skies over Coori.

By the time Angelica walked in Leah had completed a whole section with balloons rising into the sky like a spring of giant fresh-water bubbles. The day before she had painted in Angel's surrealistic idea of floating umbrellas and several large silver trophy cups copied from those in Jake's study. There was considerably more to be done but she had made a great start. The four-foot section of the rear wall was to become a billabong featuring the magnificent species of waterlilies unique to the Channel Country and Coori station.

This was Leah's wish as the waterlily flower was the totemic ancestor of her coastal tribe. Connecting billabong to sky from the drawing board design would be a range of amethyst hills.

"That's coming along beautifully, Leah," Angelica called, thrilled by Leah's progress. It confirmed Leah's talent and Angelica's faith in her. She had since seen a large portfolio of Leah's work full of wonderful imagery and the fantasy of aboriginal mythology as well as Coori landscapes filtered through aboriginal eyes. It was a style, entirely natural, that combined elements of both worlds. Aboriginal culture and that of the white man's.

To Angelica's thinking in terms of commercial success, it seemed to give Leah's work an edge. Whoever had given Leah lessons—a nun at the mission—knew what she was about.

"I'm happy, Miss," Leah said, a sense of workmanship and pride her normal demeanour these days.

"So you should be," Angelica said admiringly. "You're going to make a name for yourself with this."

"Mr. McCord likes it." Leah grinned. "He said he can't wait for me to start paintin' the horses. He loves horses."

"So do I," said Angelica, who continued diligently with her early morning and late-afternoon lessons, enjoying herself immensely while she was at it. She had a marvellously helpful teacher, a complete professional, who freely admitted she had a good natural seat and good hands. This made his job that much easier.

Leah's design featured three polo ponies and riders during play. The front rider was to be clearly recognisable as Jake wearing his Number 3 jersey, the position for a team's most experienced player and usually the captain. This was Leah's idea.

Angelica stayed on for a while, making sure to praise little Kylee for her efforts, delighted the child had inherited her mother's talent. Rather than return to the lounge and Dinah Campbell she thought she'd go in search of Jake. She knew from their morning conversation he was schooling the best of the latest pool of brumbies. She had never heard him use the term "breaking in." It would be interesting to see him and Dinah together. That wouldn't happen until a pre-dinner drink unless Dinah took it into her head to find Jake, as well. It couldn't have been more obvious she had little in common with Stacy and Gillian while Stacy and Gillian appeared to find Dinah exhausting.

What of Jake? Angelica steeled herself for the answer. She took the Pajero in the direction of the Four Mile where she knew there were holding yards following the chain of billabongs. Coori station seemed to go on forever. She had only seen its boundaries from the air. A lake-size expanse of lagoon looked wonderfully inviting shimmering through the trees. It appeared deep enough but the water must have contracted because it was surrounded by a wide sandy beach. Reed beds abounded and the ubiquitous waterlily. In this particular lagoon it was the lavender-blue of the lotus lily sacred to the ancient Egyptians. For as long as she could remember there had always been talk of an ancient Egyptian presence in Australia especially in the tropical north. The beautiful lotus lily was native to both countries.

Slowing her vehicle, she first heard then saw a small waterfall cascading down the worn-smooth rock face at the back of the lagoon. And this was drought, except for that one miraculous downpour. She wondered what the waterfall would be like in times of flood or the wet years when probably it would be huge. A tree stretched its long branches over the lagoon and she thought it would be a marvellous place for the children on the station to hang a rope to jump from. Just as she thought it she saw an old rope dangling from one of the branches and laughed aloud thinking someone had already had the bright idea.

When she arrived at the Four Mile she found Jake working his magic on a wild stallion. She parked in the shade and walked quietly across the lightly grassed space, her face alight with interest. Three stockmen had taken up learning positions on the opposite side of the railed enclosure and she waved to them, watching them doff their dusty wide-brimmed hats before she found herself a nice comfortable spot around the fence.

Jake glanced at her briefly, but he didn't speak, clearly focused on the job. She, however, felt a sense of longing that was like an actual weight. She was, she realised, in so deep she craved the sight of him. The brumby looked a fine specimen, not poor at all for its life lived in the semi-arid desert fringe. She knew brumbies could become useful and tractable working horses. She wasn't sure what stage Jake was at, or indeed what the stages were, but the horse wasn't bucking or pawing the ground. It looked entirely controllable, probably due to Jake's unique skill.

Eventually as she watched with great interest, the horse was saddled and Jake mounted quietly, gently urging the animal forward. She supposed a considerable amount of work had gone into the lead-up processes for the horse to accept the saddle then the rider. Maybe the final schooling? The horse moved off at a steady controlled pace.

Moments later Jake dismounted, handing over the reins to one of the stockmen and calling a few instructions. Apparently it was someone else's turn to try their hand. In another enclosure a distance away she could see a number of horses milling, their hooves raising a bright rust-red cloud of dust. Jake had already told her large numbers of brumbies roamed the vast Outback stations.

He loped towards her, his lean powerful frame so extraordinarily graceful in its movements she felt a great thrust of sexual excitement, which extended from her heart through her groin to her legs. He was magnificent. She couldn't help but imagine what it would be like to lie beside him in a big soft beautiful bed!

"This is a pleasant surprise," he drawled, thinking if they were on their own he couldn't be responsible for what happened.

"I'm only sorry I didn't come sooner." Her smile was a

ray of sunshine in her vivid face. "I take it that horse has been through any number of stages to allow you to ride it like that?"

He pushed his akubra lazily further down over his eyes. "Ma'am, you take it right. Schooling horses is a job I really enjoy. I find it pleasurable and a challenge. We don't need as many station horses as we used to. Helicopters and motor bikes have taken over the musters, but I like to put the best of the brumbies to use. The rest can run free. It's time-consuming, this so-called business of breaking horses in. Coori adopted the British method of breaking horses in from the earliest days. The big difference was that over there horses were used to humans from the beginning and so were more tractable and well-behaved. Our brumbies roamed a vast wilderness and never saw a single human soul. Consequently they're damned wild. And fierce."

"So a gentleman in Britain could walk right up to an un-schooled horse and pat its nose while an Outback man had a far more dangerous time of it."

"You bet!" He yanked at the red bandana around his strong bronzed throat. "If they ever managed to catch the strongest and fleetest. A wild horse's response to a direct approach would be to bolt like merry hell. In my grandfather's day when he was still a young man his best friend, a fine horseman, was killed on the station. He made the fatal mistake of walking away from a brumby that was being broken in. The horse lashed out with its hinds legs, smashing his arm, shoulder and finally near caved in the side of his head."

"How terrible!" Angelica said weakly.

"Horses are unpredictable creatures." He shrugged. "They can bite, rear or strike savagely with their front and rear feet. That's why good horsemen take pride in their ability to ride any horse with safety and facility."

"Have you been thrown?" She looked back at him with the greatest sense of pleasure.

He sent her an amused glance. "I've taken my share of

falls, but strangely I've never broken anything. There's an expertise in taking a fall as well. As for you, you're making an improvement every day.''

She executed a little bow. ''Thank you. I have a top-rate teacher. You're surprisingly patient.''

One bronzed brow shot up. ''What do you mean, surprisingly?'' he scoffed.

''You're a man who doesn't suffer fools gladly.''

His golden gaze narrowed over her. ''I can't believe you're calling yourself a fool.''

''You know what I mean. Anyway I'm very grateful to you. When I go home I'm going to keep up my riding.''

In an exquisitely gentle gesture that surprised the both of them he reached out to tilt up her chin, her skin petals to his touch. ''And what if you can't bear to leave me?''

''I have to return.'' It came out in a sigh. God, how she wanted to stay.

''So we're just having an affair?'' He looked deeply into her dark eyes, as he fought against the overwhelming urge to gather her into his arms.

''Are we? There's been no sex.'' A bittersweet little smile touched her lips.

''I thought that was your idea.'' His tone was half mocking, half quizzical, but he was watching her very intently.

''I want you to treat me differently to every other woman you've ever known in your life,'' she burst out so emotively she had to turn her head away to regain her composure. ''And speaking of girlfriends...'' After a moment she swung back, her voice even again. ''Dinah Campbell has arrived. I've never known a woman who piloted her own plane.''

''Dinah's had a licence since she was eighteen,'' he said, jamming his hands into his jeans' pockets just in case he reached for her again. Damn, he could scarcely keep his hands off her. ''The Piper was her father's twenty-first birthday present to her.''

''Which makes it remarkably easy to pop in and out,'' she pointed out dryly.

"Light aircraft is a way of life out here, Angelica. Not a luxury, a necessity."

"You don't have to say a word more. I just find it fascinating."

"And how did you find Dinah?"

She automatically braced. "Like an aristocrat out of those old British movies, ordering the servants about."

"In other words, a bit of a snob?"

"Exactly. I will say she's very attractive. You've told me she's very competent, as well—no doubt as a bed mate—what interests me is, apart from the fact you probably played naked as little children, what attracted you to her?"

"Jealous?" His hands came free to trap her. He caught a long coil of hair and wound it around his wrist.

"Not yet. Mind you I could be." She tugged back a little, but he didn't let go. "So, what went wrong?"

"You mean, between Dinah and me?" He flicked his wrist over, drawing her closer.

"Stop stalling, McCord. I'll get around to questioning you about your other affairs later. For now, just the imperious Dinah."

"I don't like the way she treats people, either, which echoes your concerns."

"Outback aristocrat and all that?"

"Dinah would be a snob anywhere," he said wryly, and let the length of her curly hair go, watching it bounce back. "Outback people are generally very down to earth."

"Perhaps I'll find she's down to earth when I get to know her better. I certainly wouldn't like to jeopardise your relationship with her."

"We're friends. I don't want to make love to her. Is that plain enough?"

"But you do know what she's like in bed? Average. Good. Sensational?"

He shifted to lean back against the fence, elegant even in a slouch. "Mind your own business, Angel Face."

Her brow lifted. "Understand it is my business. We're

already involved. To some degree anyway. I'll try again.
What about marriage to Dinah? Have you ever thought about
it? It would be a union of two Outback dynasties, after all.''

"Except I want you."

"Why? Do you think you could tell me?" Now she stared
near pleadingly into his golden mesmeric eyes.

Why didn't he? He had a deep underlying wish to do so
but always there was the emotional hurdle. "Well, you're not
exactly ugly," he evaded, taking the easy way out. "Not
stupid, either. You're amazingly sexy. I can't get you out of
my head."

"Or into your bed," she pointed out quietly.

"Isn't this some kind of foreplay?" There was challenge
in his tone. Didn't she make the world come alive for him?

"It worked for Anne Boleyn." She smiled.

"Ah, but wasn't she the one who lost her head?"

"Admittedly she had her problems." She glanced at her
watch. "Well, stimulating as this conversation is, I must tear
myself away. I promised Stacy I'd return for lunch."

"Then I'll walk you to the car," he said in a gallant manner. "Have you everything settled for the weekend?"

"Everything but the weather. There's nothing for you to
worry about. We're all going to have a marvellous day. I
can't wait to see you play polo. I expect you're absolutely
super?"

"I can't lie." His answer was droll. He opened the door
for her. "Have you ever been in a steady relationship,
Angel?"

She was sensitive to the gravity behind their habitual ban-
ter. "What's steady?" she asked. "More than a week?"

"When are you going to be serious? Or is it too much to
expect?"

"You should t-talk!" She almost stuttered at his arrogance. "The two of us need to work on some issues."

His smile was beautiful, maddening unsettling. "Okay."

"Look, I'm normal." She drew a breath. "I'm twenty-five

until my next birthday. I've had a couple of fairly steady relationships.''

''Do you want to get married?''

''Of course I do.'' She stared at him, baffled.

''What, years from now? You, the career girl with your beautiful face in magazines and on TV? Hell, they could even want you for the movies. When exactly do you plan to marry? The near future? Or is it career first?''

''Oh go to hell!'' She'd give her career away for him anyday. Taut as a wire, she rushed past him to get into the vehicle, only their bodies were so irresistibly bent to each other, her breasts crushed against his chest. She swung into the driver's seat, hot-cheeked, aroused nipples straining against her T-shirt. ''I hope to marry just as soon as I can,'' she said, working herself into a minifury, ''but you can bet your life it won't be to anyone as insufferable as you!''

Her remark led to one blazing, retaliatory kiss through the window. It was passion perfectly balanced with punishment.

''Know what, Angel?'' His golden eyes mocked. ''You might find it hard to get insufferable old me out of your system.''

The hell was she'd come to that conclusion herself. Angelica drove off in a flurry of red dust, anger and a crazy rapture roaring through her head.

Damn that man, McCord!

CHAPTER NINE

By THE Friday before the polo final and the gala ball, Dinah Campbell was still with them. In fact, as Stacy put it, she'd as good as moved in. She had brought all necessary luggage with her—including her evening dress and possibly a tiara. As she pointed out in the time-honoured tradition of Coori she had come for a prolonged stay. Coori boasted many bedrooms from the old days when relatives and friends who made the long journey stayed for some time, so there was no difficulty accommodating her. She was, however, visibly put out when she discovered that Angelica occupied the very best guest suite, the one she considered her suite. Obviously she truly believed, if no one else did, that she was going to marry Jake.

"She's not happy!" Gillian conveyed to Angelica, then relaxed into a fit of the giggles. "What about you move out?"

"But, Gilly, I think she expects me to."

"She's a stuck-up cow!" Gilly returned irreverently.

What was heart-warming was to see Gillian in particular come out of her shell so far as her interaction with Dinah was concerned. Even Stacy, who wasn't given to tart remarks, had come out with a surprising few after being on the receiving end of Dinah's curiously loaded comments. It was almost a form of heckling, Angel thought, fired up by protectiveness. Basically Dinah was a bitch. That was until Jake walked into the house. Then a great transformation took place. Dinah turned herself into the woman every man wants. She set out to charm him. She became all warmth and caring, eager to share station concerns, indicating she was the ideal choice for a wife.

At the dinner table, always beautifully turned out, she rose effortlessly to sparkling conversation, prompting him to tell stories of the many, many days, months, years they had spent together, all the while hanging on his every word.

Then, when Jake was out of the house she reverted to strutting her stuff, expelling oddly cutting little comments and upsetting Clary with questions as how the house was run, as if it were only a matter of time before Clary would be dumped and she would reign as mistress of a grand station. Sometimes Angelica had to place herself bodily between Clary and Dinah in case Clary, who had a fiery Irish temper, had armed herself with a sheaf of kitchen knives.

As for Angelica herself! She had to contend with endless interruptions and interventions as Dinah, to Angelica's intense irritation, gave herself the role of supervisor and interrogator. "Two heads are better than one!" she would say with a grating false laugh, coming to stare over Angelica's shoulder at some plan Angelica and Clary had stitched up until Angelica put her palms down firmly over the paper.

"Of course I could have done this and saved Jake a lot of money, but he was a little bit worried I might tire myself out. You're such a big strong woman." At this point she stared fixedly at Angelica's bosom as though it were massive.

Dinah, in fact, became so annoying Angelica and Jake had a brief exchange of words before he left the homestead on the Friday morning. "Look, she's your ex-girlfriend and she's really bugging me," Angelica cried, catching him as he ran down the front steps. "I have so much to do and she's a nuisance."

Jake, who was actually fed up with Dinah himself and worried about one of his prize beasts, rounded on the indignant Angelica. "Kill her," he said, golden eyes flashing.

"You're saying you're agreeable?"

"I'm saying I'm too damned busy to listen to this, Angel," he answered brusquely. "You're a smart girl. There's nothing wrong with your tongue, either. Tell her off."

"Oh, right! The only person off the hook is you," she said

tartly. "God, what a difference when you hove into sight. Okay I'll handle it," she called loudly as he gave her a back-handed wave and moved off with great purpose and energy. "Next time you can get somebody else in."

It all came to a head around noon, as the sky turned blue-black. Great thunder-heads streaming tails behind them like comets were building up in the sky. Angelica, hot and bothered, returned to the house from her inspection of the marquees already set up around the polo ground worried sick rain would ruin everything. They had all worked so hard, including the station hands Jake put at her disposal. Their number included Charlie who had kept them all laughing and Gillian especially happy.

Now this! Even if it didn't rain they could experience a wild windstorm or a dust storm that could bring the marquees down, tip over all the tables and chairs and rip the bunting to shreds. She didn't like Jake out in this, either, although she knew perfectly well he had lived with these extraordinary climatic conditions all his life.

She had only set foot in the entrance hall when a distant crack of thunder rolled around the hill country and little Kylee descended on her with a yelp. "It's all right, sweetheart." Angelica bent to the child, hugging her, thinking she was frightened of the thunder when Dinah suddenly appeared looking positively dragon-like.

"That child again!" she fumed. "I told her not to run around the house—so many valuable things…the Chinese porcelains alone—but she doesn't take the slightest notice. She behaves very badly. There's no way I would allow her or any other willful child in the house. She simply doesn't know what it is to be careful. Small wonder!"

"Do you mind, Dinah?" Angelica interrupted the tirade. "She's frightened of the thunder."

Kylee looked up at Angelica, small face wearing a frown. "No, I'm not, Miss. I'm frightened of her. But you're here now."

"Oh, yes, Mary Poppins!" Dinah took a crack at Angelica.

"Surely you realise there's really something very negligent about all this," she pointed out, not unreasonably had she used a different tone. But there she stood, the next mistress of Coori, guarding her future possessions. That was how she saw it in her own mind at least. "And if you don't mind my saying so—" as though anyone could stop her "—you shouldn't have put this tree here," she told Angelica as if she had no sense at all. "It's the wrong place entirely. It obstructs the traffic. One would have thought you'd know better."

"'Cause we like it," Kylee suddenly yelled in a voice extraordinarily shrill for one so tiny. "You can't touch it, lady. I'll tell Mr. Jake on yuh."

"Is that child actually speaking to me?" Dinah hissed her disbelief.

"It would appear so." Angel refrained from laughing because Kylee had been rude.

"Apologise to Miss Campbell, Kylee."

"No I ain't," said Kylee with almost adult disgust.

This time Angelica was forced to smother a laugh. "Well, no one can say I didn't try. Perhaps you can leave Kylee alone, Dinah," she suggested. "I'll keep an eye on her." She used Dinah's name when Dinah made a point of never using hers.

"Surely it's her mother's job?" Dinah's rasping tones were threaded with disapproval. "Whatever is she doing in the Great Hall? It must be clean by now?"

"She's paintin'," Kylee spoke up, pressing her heated face against Angelica's hand. "Don't want you there!"

Angelica bent down to the child, who apparently, for all Jake's concerns, feared no one. "You're being very rude, you know, Kylee," she chided softly.

"Sorry, Miss."

"Am I missing something here?" Dinah looked as though Kylee's words had set off an alarm.

"Just keep out of the Great Hall, Dinah, if you don't mind," Angelica asked. Leah was putting the finishing touches to her mural, which was so exactly what Angelica wanted and she didn't want Leah upset in any way.

"Since when have you been giving orders?" Dinah looked at Angelica with a twisted smile. "I'm a close friend of the family. Who exactly are you, when it's all said and done."

"She's Miss," Kylee yelled, clutching at Angelica like two sisters sticking together. "Go away, lady."

"This has gone quite far enough," Dinah cried promptly. "That child is truly out of hand."

Her expression was so outraged Angelica found herself losing her cool.

"God, Dinah, when was the last time you were nice to her? It might come as a surprise but it's not your job to chastise Kylee."

"Indeed it is, thank you very much. It'll be the day when some little aboriginal mite dares shout at me. It's not done."

"Say sorry, Kylee," Angelica prompted once more, "it is rude to shout at people." Kylee really hadn't been too respectful.

"I'm hot," Kylee said instead. "Can I go for a swim?"

"Watch out, she'll probably want to go in the homestead pool," Dinah said in her most sarcastic tone.

"That's an idea." Angelica swung the child up into her arms. "You're not the only one, Kylee, who feels like cooling off."

By four o'clock Angelica was convinced they were in for torrential rain. She'd already had the men move all the tables and chairs they'd so carefully set up into the shelter of the two large marquees. Everyone had agreed there seemed to be a wetness in the air, which meant a chance of rain. Storm-clouds now covered the great vault of the sky entirely.

She and Clary were left standing on the verandah staring up at the heavens that periodically flashed bursts of light like someone was running from one heavenly room to the other, throwing switches. "This is going to ruin everything," Angelica groaned, easing her T-shirt from her damp midriff.

"Try not to worry, love." Clary, equally worried, did her best to comfort her. "It might come to nothing. I've seen it happen too many times before."

"But what if the wind gets up?" Angelica said.

"The marquees will be all right, love. It's not as though we're expecting a cyclone."

"What about a dust storm?" Angelica fretted. She had never seen one but she had seen pictures of Outback dust storms and they were horrendous!

"Look, love, whatever happens, happens." Clary, who had seen it all, flood drought, dust storms, the lot, spoke philosophically.

"I know. It's just that we've all worked so hard, Clary. Stacy and Gilly have really pulled their weight, too."

"They've done well," Clary agreed, surprised and pleased at the way they'd all worked together. "You've made it so much fun for them. They haven't had a lot of fun."

"Not with a family friend like Dinah Campbell around." Angelica leaned closer to Clary to whisper, "Where is she now, for goodness' sake?"

"Gone after Mr. Jake, my darling," Clary told her dryly. "That's what she does. Go after Mr. Jake."

"Do you reckon she might get him?" Angelica asked. God, what a dismal thought.

"Reckon you might if you want the job," Clary shocked her by saying. "It isn't exactly what you're used to out here. You're on your way to being a celebrity all right."

"Don't you think I'd fit in?" Angelica, who had no desire to be a celebrity, turned to Clary with a very serious expression on her face.

Clary threw back her head and laughed. "Listen, love, you fitted in from day one. You've been good for us all. Like a cure. I see the way Mr. Jake lights up when you're coming. I hear the way he calls you Angel."

"That doesn't mean he won't forget me when I'm gone."

"It could be up to you, love," Clary mused. "You're the

one with the city career. Mr. Jake can't leave here. This is his heritage. He'll never abandon it.''

"I couldn't think of him elsewhere," Angelica answered simply. "He's not only the most committed, he has to be the best-looking cattleman on earth."

"You're not kiddin'!" Clary laughed with almost motherly pride. "Now I've got things to do. You can't keep fretting about this storm. It's either going to come to nothing or all hell will break loose."

"So why doesn't Jake come home?" Angelica asked anxiously as another drum roll of thunder echoed around the hills.

"He's been used to this his whole life. Don't you go worryin' about him. He can look after himself."

But Angelica felt as edgy as a cat on a hot tin roof. She couldn't follow Clary inside. Instead she ran down the steps intent on making one more circuit of the polo grounds....

When Jake did return to the homestead fifteen minutes later, he went in search of Angelica, knowing she would be concerned about the storm and its possible effect on all her hard work and planning. Even nearing sundown it was still scorchingly hot but there was a wet smell in the air. Personally having studied the sky he didn't think it would amount to much, but to a city person, like Angelica, it could be very frightening. These storm fronts, messengers of the monsoon season made everyone cranky. It was a case of all the drama without the relief of a drop of rain.

Tomorrow they would all gather for the final of the polo cup. It would be played in fierce heat but it had all been done before. People were used to it. He was prepared to take a very large bet it would be played under peacock-blue cloudless skies. He found Stacy and Gillian in the plant-filled conservatory at the rear of the house. Both of them turned smiling faces to him.

"Hi! Where's everyone?"

"If you mean Angelica, and I think you do, she's with

Clary.'' Stacy smiled. ''If you mean Dinah, she's in her room. She said the heat was giving her a headache. She tries to spend as little time with us as she can.''

''The next time she wants to come, put her off,'' Jake suggested.

''She's just so hard to put off.'' Stacy sighed.

''Maybe not if you try. I think I'll find Angel. She must be worried this storm will build into heavy rain.''

''Yes. She's so much at home here you forget she's a city girl,'' Stacy said. ''That was awfully nice of her getting the right evening dresses flown in to us. She must have described us exactly to her friend. Colouring, sizes, everything. They fit perfectly.''

''And it gives us a great chance to shine!'' Gillian showed her delight. ''Maybe Charlie will really fall in love with me. Up to date he hasn't.''

''You've got Charlie on the brain,'' her mother complained. ''Admittedly he is a fine young man, but Ty Caswell thinks the world of you.''

''I already know that, Mum.''

''Personally I think Ty suits you better,'' offered Jake. The very last thing he wanted was for Gillian to know heartbreak when Charlie went home. And that's what he was going to do when his big adventure was over.

Angel wasn't with Clary. She wasn't anywhere in the house. She wasn't in the Great Hall, either. He stopped long enough to admire Leah's mural, amazed at how good it was and the speed with which she had done it. Angel, being an angel, had given him her considered opinion, amounting to a little lecture, that Leah should be given a helping hand to relocate in Sydney where there would be more scope for her talents. Importantly, too, there were service and support groups within the aboriginal community in the city. Good aboriginal art was much sought after, both at home and abroad. Leah was good. And she had her dress-designing skills with ambitions thrown in. He sort of liked the idea of

sponsoring her and little Kylee. God knows, after what Leah
had suffered she deserved a helping hand.

A quick check confirmed the four-wheel drive had gone.
Probably she had gone out to the polo grounds again, unable
to settle. She could even want to camp out there tonight. He
tried not to think of them both in one sleeping bag together.
He was sick with wanting her. Sick of all his primitive urges.
They were forever lapping at his senses. Willpower wouldn't
work. He had fallen madly in love with Angelica De Campo.
And faster than he thought possible. How was that for a swift
slide into spellbound? Yet would a woman like that bury her
beauty and talents in the remoteness of an Outback station?
Maybe she was totally unattainable as an Outback wife. But
not as a woman. He knew what he could do to her once he
got her in his arms. Create a world within a world for them…

He was halfway to the grounds riding one of the station
motor bikes when he spotted the Pajero coming over the crest
of a ridge. It was travelling wickedly fast and he began to
curse with anxiety. He couldn't bear to see her crash.

Slow down, girl. What's the race?

Another minute more and he knew. Smoke.

"God!" In among the spiralling column of dirty grey
smoke he saw a shooting flame then a great shower of sparks.
He realised instantly what had happened. A tree had ignited.
He had lived through years when the station was dotted with
spot fires. The wind was coming from the direction of the
blaze. He caught a blast of heat and aromatic burning gum
oil in his face. The danger zone was about a kilometre from
the polo grounds. It was uncanny the way fire ran in lines
and trees lined the ridge. With the wind behind the bushfire
it could just miss the polo grounds. Unless the wind shifted.
He opened up the throttle, slamming down hard as he tore
up and over the rising ground until he met up with Angelica.

She brought the four-wheel drive to a shuddering halt,
jumping out, calling to him as she ran. "Jonathon, thank
God, you're here. Lightning hit a tree. It absolutely exploded.

The whole thing ignited right in front of my eyes. It was so scary. I was parked under it only a few moments before.''

He raced to her, grabbed her arms, held her fast. ''Are you okay?'' He searched her face, seeing anxiety but not a flicker of panic in her great dark eyes.

''I'm fine.'' She was now. She felt the force of his strength and inner energy. ''I don't know about your vehicle. A chunk of burning wood hit the roof hard but it must have fallen away.''

''I'm not worried about the damned vehicle,'' he said tautly. ''I was worried about you. All I want you to do now is get the men. It won't take them long to spot the flames. We want the water truck, backpacks, hessian bags, buckets, anything. They know the drill. We can't let this spread and there's no time.''

''I'll get them,'' she said, already on the run. ''What are you going to do?''

''I'm going to take a closer look.''

''Be careful!'' she yelled, her voice competing against the thunder. Even as she spoke another tree ignited, the canopy of branches throwing up great multi-coloured sparks like a fireworks display. If it weren't so frightening it would have been beautiful.

''Go on, Angel. Move it,'' he ordered, pretty shortly.

She didn't waste another second. She leapt into the vehicle and took off, reaching the compound in record time. The men were already alerted, swiftly going about their business. Everything they could use had been assembled.

''You don't have to come, Angelica.'' She and Charlie had become quite friendly, now he made a beeline for her, an odd excitement on his young handsome face. ''It could be bad up there. Really bad if the fire takes hold.''

''I'm coming all the same,'' she said. ''I want to be there. I want to help.''

''Then you'd better take this.'' He shoved a scarf into her hand. ''Put it over your face once we're up there. You won't want to breathe in the smoke.''

"Thanks, Charlie. Take care." Her voice resonated with concern. She watched him swing onto the side of the water truck equipped with barrels of water and a big yellow fire hose. Travelling towards their destination they all saw the fires take hold. Burn-offs had already taken place over most of the vast station during the Dry but the line of trees on the ridge had been left as a windbreak. Now the canopies were on fire, looking for all the world like a line of streetlights at night.

When they arrived at the fire front the men threw themselves into action, but Jake, once he caught sight of Angelica, strode towards her, his dynamic face grim. "This is no place for you." Already the wind was blasting embers across the dusty clearing. "Go back to the house."

"I can help," she protested, drawing on her own inner strength. "I'm another pair of hands. I won't get too close to it."

He held her a hair's-breadth away, staring down into her eyes. "Don't think for a minute it can't get close to you," he warned, lean body taut, nerves tense.

"Why don't you let me take one of those backpacks?" she shouted over the frightening crackle of the flames and the continuous roar of thunder. "I'm strong. Please, Jonathon, let me stay. I don't want you to be alone."

"You're not counting the men?" Abruptly he gave a crooked smile, a flash of white teeth in a smoke-grimed face. "Okay. Grab one. You know how to pump the water? But the moment I tell you to go, you'll go, understand?"

"I promise." She was inordinately pleased he trusted her to do something. She jumped to pick up a backpack while Jake strode away to the water truck.

Charlie surged forward to help her put the backpack on. "I wouldn't miss this," he told her, bending close so she could hear him.

"You must be mad." She recognised his excitement.

He lifted his blond head to scan the lurid sky. "My problem is, I have to have excitement. Will you just look at that spectacle!'' Billowing black clouds, shot through with silver and livid green, made a fantastic backdrop for the searing orange-gold flames.

''After all the work we put in there, I'd say it was heading towards the polo grounds.''

''Then we shouldn't be standing here talking,'' she clipped off.

''Okay, ma'am.'' Charlie saluted her with his devil-may-care grin. ''I like your spirit!''

It would have been a miracle if the skies had opened and sent down torrential rain. Only miracles didn't happen on demand. For three hours the fires continued to rage, jumping from tree to tree, the branches falling in fiery clumps causing ripples of tiny flames to skitter across the dry grass and smouldering leaves. All of them worked with their clothes, wet and steamy, clinging to them, for they had all doused themselves with the hoses. Once a small branch like a flaming torch fell not a metre from Angelica and she bit back a scream. That was close! She could have taken it on the head or the shoulder and been badly burned. She felt a wave of relief.

Jake's glistening blackened face appeared close to her. ''That's it, Angel. Go,'' he ordered harshly. ''For God's sake, that branch nearly hit you.'' He made a grab for her hand. ''Come on.'' Her hand was so oily, so grimy, it slithered out of his.

''We're getting there, aren't we?'' She took a long, dry, painful swallow. It seemed to her they were, though the very air was burning.

''I don't want you here. You've done well. I'm proud of you, but you can't stay. Get going.''

''All right.'' She turned away obediently, as she saw him agitated and angry. Now she was feeling dizzy, dying for one gulp of water.

''Please be careful,'' she begged, her heart in her eyes.

"I'll wait for you." She realised she was so exhausted she was on the verge of tears.

"I'll be okay," he shouted, turning to put out a spot fire on the ground with a few powerful sweeps of a hessian bag. "I'm not telling you one more time, Angel. Go."

She did just that, finding her way back to her vehicle. Her body felt like it was made of lead. Her mind was full of anxiety and an unfamiliar sensation she knew was pure panic. She was bound to Jake McCord in the most powerful way. She loved him. His life meant everything.

Angelica climbed wearily into the driver's seat and began to pray.

"Whatever possessed you to go up there?"

She'd only just arrived back at the homestead when Dinah thrust her face through the open window. Obviously she felt no need to ask Angelica how she was or if the fire was coming under control. The big thing was to tear down the front stairs the moment she spotted the four-wheel drive coming in so she could be first to ask the questions. "Don't you know anything about danger?" she scolded. "I bet Jake didn't thank you for getting yourself involved."

"Got a message for you," Angelica said laconically, opening out the door so smartly Dinah was forced to jump back. "He did." She resisted the urge to give Dinah a good shove.

"I don't believe that for a minute," Dinah gasped, staggering back. "I'm sure he told you to go away."

Angelica nodded wearily. "He did in the end, but I know I was of help."

"You could have placed the men in danger." Dinah continued the attack, uncaring of Angel's visible exhaustion. "They don't need a woman to get in the middle of things. The risks are too great. The men are trained."

"Go away, Dinah," Angelica said very quietly. Too quietly. Before the remnants of her self-control floated off into the night.

"If you actually cared," Dinah told her piously, sounding

like a woman with a great capacity for emotional involvement, "Stacy and Gillian were very worried about you."

"I take it you weren't."

Silence. Then... "I knew Jake would send you on your
way." Dinah was not a pretty sight in her jealousy and anger.

"Then he took his time about it. I'd say I've been up there
two hours and more." Angelica normally so light-footed,
dragged her steps as she started towards the house.

"Either you'd do anything to get Jake's attention or you're
insane." Dinah came after her, her mind suddenly filled with
doomed dreams.

"Anything else you'd like to add?" Angelica turned so
abruptly Dinah almost slammed into her.

"Yes." Dinah's green eyes were twin daggers as she
threw down the challenge. Now was a good time. Everything
being as rotten as it was. "Just make sure you don't try to
come between Jake and me."

Angelica surveyed Dinah from her superior height. "If you
disappeared off the face of the earth I bet you he wouldn't
notice."

Dinah lost it. "I don't give a stuff what you think," she
said furiously. "You'll be gone the day after the Christmas
party. We'll never see you again."

"When I've already got Jake to sign me up for his birthday
party?"

"Wha-a-t?" Dinah visibly recoiled.

"You heard. Jake is starting to get a real appreciation for
my talents."

"All the sex appeal?" Dinah sneered, almost demented
with jealousy. "Slut. I bet there are a lot of wild stories about
you."

"You wish. Then you could take them all to Jake.
Personally I have no idea what slut means. But if you asked
me what a super-bitch was I could tell you."

Up on the verandah Stacy and Gillian peered into the night
anxiously. It had been a long worrying time and Dinah hadn't
made things better with her incessant criticisms of Angelica.

"Oh, we're so glad you're back, Angelica, dear." Stacy flew down the steps the instant Angelica came into sight. "How's it going up there?" She lifted her eyes to the illuminated ridge. "It doesn't seem anywhere near as threatening, thank God."

"I'd say they were getting over the top of things at last," Angelica told her as they stood at the bottom of the steps. "Lighting hit a tree. That's what started it off."

"Angie, Angie, are you all right?" Now Gillian appeared, running down the short flight of steps to join them. "Why, you poor thing, you look exhausted. We would have been out of our minds with worry only we knew Jake was with you. You're very brave to have stayed. Fire is terrifying." She stared up into Angelica's face, thinking her a heroine.

"I'm as tough as old leather boots," Angelica laughed, when she felt more like slipping to her knees.

"Or too stupid to know better," Dinah suggested harshly, pleased Miss De Campo looked decidedly unsexy for once.

"Dinah, please don't! Now's not the time," Stacy begged, utterly dismayed by Dinah's attitude. Gillian, however, was wrought up enough to reach out and give Dinah a good push.

"You just won't shut up, will you, Dinah?" she said. "Leave Angie alone. Who do you think you are anyway? You treat Mum and I like dirt in our own home. You think Jake's in love with you and he's not. For God's sake, get a grip."

Dinah, fell back, utterly shocked, groping for words. "I can't believe you did that, Gilly," she said, feeling her shoulder like Gillian had broken the bone.

"No, you thought I was too much of a wimp," Gillian said. "Father practically made sure I was, though he was hospitable enough to you. Both of you rotten snobs. Leave Angie alone. She's our friend. Can't you see she's reeling on her feet?"

"Maybe it will teach her a lesson," Dinah cried the harder, thoroughly startled by Gillian's growth in self-confidence. She flinched in faked pain. "I'll be telling Jake just how rude you've been to me, Gilly." she threatened. "I don't know why you should attack your poor father, either. He was quite charming to me."

"Oh, sure!" Gillian snorted. "Father just exuded charm. You could have told him all about my rudeness for all I care, because boy, it was worth it. Your rudeness on the other hand has gone on long enough."

"Gilly, darling, Dinah is our guest," Stacy wailed, wondering where it was all going to end.

"She invited herself."

"So is Jake complaining?" Dinah asked. "I think you're getting very much above yourself, Gilly."

Gillian threw back her head and laughed. "That's priceless coming from you. Anyway it's Angie who needs our attention."

"Yes, dear. Come inside," Stacy pleaded, all but wringing her hands. "You'll feel much better after a long shower." She looked back towards the ridge where billows of smoke still filled the dark night. "I think the fire has gone as far as it's going to," she said with great hope. "There's never a dull moment around here. We've got our big day tomorrow."

"Put it off," said Dinah with considerable disdain. The very last thing she wanted was for Angelica's efforts to amount to a great success.

"Put it off?" Both McCord women looked at her in disbelief. "That's impossible. It looks like Jake and the men have the fire under control," Stacy pointed out. "We have to go ahead. People will expect it. I'm sure Jake will want us to."

"Besides, we've all worked ourselves silly," Angelica said, having taken up a position against the stone pillar for support.

"So, dear," said Stacy most affectionately, "when are you going to take your shower?"

"Just as soon as I can get myself around the back," Angelica replied. "I can't go through the front door like this." She glanced down at her ruined shirt and jeans.

"Not when you're positively dripping dirty water," said Dinah with a kind of relish. "I think I'll be the one to greet Jake when he returns."

It was nearing midnight before Jake and his team felt confident to return to the home compound. They had watched and waited for any sign of a flare-up. Then around eleven they had a patch of rain. It was nothing approaching the substantial downpour they wanted, just an erratic scatter of heavy drops. Still, it was enough to dampen the ground and allow the temperature to drop.

The lights were on at the homestead. He expected Stacy and Gilly would be waiting. They had never been active women like Angel who wanted to pitch in there and help. His father would have forbidden them anyway. Both of them were frightened of the spot fires that broke out somewhere on the station every summer. Even then, Coori was prepared. Not only prepared but blessed. It had its interlocking system of creeks, bores, billabongs, lagoons, swamps. Wypanga Creek was one of the reasons they hadn't had a roaring bushfire on their hands tonight.

Angel had certainly pulled her weight, sharing the burden with the men. He blamed himself though for not sending her home earlier. Had that flaming branch hit her she could have been badly burnt. He found the thought devastating, like a punch in the gut but she had simply shrugged it off. Still he had allowed her to get herself exhausted. Oh hell! He swore he would make it up to her.

They had their big day tomorrow and the ball at night. He knew he would be reinvigorated after a few hours' sleep. His life was a hard one, physically demanding. Angel for all her fitness and positive attitudes was a woman. No woman had the same capacity for hard physical toil as a man. She had worked her beautiful butt off tonight. He would never forget it. He would never forget the way she had looked at him, her heart in her eyes. He knew she would be waiting for him as she had promised.

For long minutes he forgot Dinah was in the house. Dinah who was supposed to be in love with him. It seemed extraordinary now he had ever considered Dinah as a wife. Even in passing. They had shared a friendship for most of their lives. His father had wanted the marriage. His father had actually approved of Dinah when he had been a man who'd approved of very few. Maybe that was one of the reasons he couldn't really cotton to Dinah. She had what was for him a terrible flaw. She lacked heart.

He had to have a serious talk with Dinah. Level with her, though he had tried often enough in the past. It only held her back to persist with this bred-in idea marriage was the only answer for people like them.

He trudged up the front steps to the verandah intending to sit a few moments with the women before taking himself off to the shower block at the rear of the house. He was far too begrimed for anything else. At his halting footsteps, Stacy, followed by Gillian then Dinah, rushed out to greet him.

Stacy had tears in her eyes. "Jake, darling. What can I say?"

She made to hug him but he drew back laughing, holding up his hands. "For God's sake, Stacy, I'm filthy!"

"Would I care?"

"Let's leave the hugs until morning." He grinned. "I must look like the survivor of a war."

To Dinah, who despite her best efforts came in third in their race to the door, he looked marvellous. A living sculpture of a wild man, his glorious hair near crow-black with stray locks of gold, his skin so darkened his eyes glittered like topaz gems. Why couldn't he see they were meant for each other? That Angelica woman was the danger. But she had taken herself off to bed, thank God, leaving her, Dinah, to support him. She could easily get rid of Stacy and Gillian. She'd done it any number of times over the years.

Only it didn't work out that way. They talked for a little while. Clary emerged in her nightclothes to check everything was all right, when suddenly Jake stood up, his manner signalling conversation was at an end for the night

"We've got a big day tomorrow," he said, already moving down the front steps. "I want it to be special. I want you girls to look your best. Which means you need your beauty sleep. I'm sorry Angel went off to bed. I wanted to thank her for everything she did."

He tried to keep his deep disappointment out of his voice. She had promised him she'd wait, but he didn't blame her in the least for finding her bed. She had a demanding day coming up. It wasn't fair to her after such a traumatic night. But still he grieved.

As the others retired, Dinah rushed forward to slide her arms around him with a rush of blood to the face. "Why don't you come to my room afterwards?" She pitched her voice low. "Let me comfort you. I so want to."

He forced a smile. "I think a good scrub is what I need, Dinah. Thanks for caring."

Dinah only nodded. "I'll leave my door unlocked," she whispered, not a whit concerned by the fact her expensive white linen shirt was now badly soiled from contact with his body.

It took him less than a minute to let himself in the rear of the house, then walk down the passageway to what the family called the "wet" room. Stacy and Gillian rarely if ever used it but the men of the house always had after a hard day in the saddle. The room contained several shower cubicles along one wall. Washbasins to the other side topped by mirrors to shave. There were cupboards that ran down the centre of the room to divide one area from the other. A long bench to sit on. It had a lot in common with a men's locker room.

Once inside, he switched on the light, before locking the door. He wouldn't put it past Dinah to chase him up. He wished for the ten thousandth time she'd find someone else. Her preoccupation with becoming mistress of Coori amounted to an obsession. He started shucking off his clothes as he rounded the line of cabinets to find towels. Tired and filthy as he was, a profound longing to see Angel swept over him.

He said her name. His special name for her. He didn't know if he said it aloud. A few seconds more and he staggered to a halt, his surprise giving way to a great surge of joy. For a moment he couldn't even believe his eyes.

There she was fast asleep on the floor. A small light above her illuminated her sleeping face. She was nearly as begrimed as he was, her beautiful skin covered in black streaks like a soldier's camouflage. Her shoulders were mashed up against a locker.

"Angel!" He squatted down. "Angel, my darling, what are you doing asleep on the floor?" He groaned with the intense feeling he couldn't hold back. "Sweetheart, wake up," he said softly, allowing his fingers to curl around her dimpled chin.

She didn't move.

He slid his arms around her, intending to pull her up, but her eyelashes flickered, then her head pitched forward a little towards his chest.

"Jonathon!" She peered up at him, slightly frowning as though she doubted he was really there. But she could see his remarkable eyes shining out of his blackened face. She reached out and placed the tips of her fingers against his cheek. Checking if he was real flesh. "You're back!" Her voice betrayed her wonder.

"It's all over. The fire's out. It's past midnight. What happened to you?"

She gave a shaky laugh, dumbstruck she hadn't made it up off the floor. "Would you believe I was going to take a shower. I was much too wet and dirty to go into the house. Here seemed the right place. I walked along to get a towel, but I must have felt dizzy for a moment. I plonked down here to recover, but I guess sleep overcame me. I don't seem to have moved."

"Well you have to move now," he said. "Let me help you. You need a shower, then bed." Gently, very gently, he wrapped his arms around her, pulling her to her feet. Even in his condition he felt driving desire and protectiveness at opposite poles. She smelt of fire, as he knew he did, but it might have been the ultimate fragrance. Her long hair was covered in a fine red dust.

"I think I've forgotten how to walk." She gave a little laugh that came out like a sob.

"I'll carry you." All he knew was, he wanted her in his arms.

"I know you're very strong but you must be dead on your feet, as well."

He wasn't. Not now. His blood was running like a molten river of lava.

"Have we got any shampoo?" she asked as he deposited her outside the first cubicle.

"We've got everything," he said with certainty. Clary made sure of it.

"You need to clean up as much as I do," she called after him with concern.

"So you take that shower recess and I'll take the one at the end. Does that fit in with your idea of the proprieties?"

"Proprieties depend on the situation at the time," she said wryly, possessed by the image of him. Even after battling a fire, soot-blackened, he was startlingly virile and handsome.

Her long hair that when the wind caught it reminded him of a raven's wing was filmed with grime. He touched her, putting the plastic bottle of shampoo into her hand. All tiredness had sloughed away from him like the skin of a desert snake. Nevertheless he got himself mobile. "You can get undressed. I promise I won't look."

"What's so terrible about a naked woman?" Exhilaration made her laugh.

"A beautiful, seductive, naked woman," he amended dryly. "You have too much power. The aborigines call it woman-magic. I discovered that when I first kissed you. What do you imagine would happen if I suddenly turned around?"

"You won't."

He heard the smile in her voice. "Why not?"

"Because you gave your word. Anyway, I'm ready."

"Good. I'll leave a couple of towels and a robe on the bench."

She turned on the taps, standing under the good strong spray that felt like a waterfall. She held up her face as exhaustion slid away with the soot. "Oh, this is heaven!" she cried, intensely aware he was only a short distance away, but not fazed by anything. For that moment—for long minutes until she was squeaky-clean—that was enough. She knew she wasn't in control of herself. She didn't care. Her heart's flutter was so pronounced she could feel it beating under her palm.

She soaped every inch of her body while she imagined soaping him. She could even feel the bronze-velvet texture of his skin. The scent of shampoo and boronia-perfumed soap surrounded her like a cloud. It was a marvellous feeling to get clean.

Finally when her ablutions were over, she slid open the door, hearing Jake humming quietly to himself as he continued to shower. He had a tuneful baritone. An old love song. She knew every word...

A profound daring swept over her. She slipped into the man's white towelling robe that was too big for her, padding softly in the direction of his shower cubicle. "Jonathon, how are you?" she called.

There was a short silence then she heard his voice. "To tell you the truth I'm longing for you to join me, though we both know what that would result in."

The vibrant tones were edged with self mockery.

"I'm already here." She placed her hand on the chrome knob, impelled to open the steam-clouded door.

The male perfection of his body stopped her in her tracks. He was an athlete, with the stature of a warrior. He was bronze all over, with no line of white anywhere. She knew the men on the station didn't give a damn about skinny-dipping after working in the intense heat. The hair at his groin was the same bright amber as the thick waves of his head. Rivulets of water ran down his noble body, a body classical in its construction. He glistened like a man freshly scrubbed.

"God, Angel!" Her impulsive action had knocked the breath from him.

"Stop me if you want to," she said, finding it impossible to move or look away.

"You know things will get out of hand?" He gave her fair warning, making no attempt to turn away from her ravished eyes.

"In that event I'm coming in." Very slowly she slid the robe down her body, allowing it to drop to the tiled floor.

Her eyes were enormous, deep and liquid, black as night. Her hair ran down her back like a bolt of satin. He stood beneath the running water transfixed by her as she had been transfixed by him. Undressed she seemed even more slender than she was in her clothes. Her shoulders were beautiful, sloping away from her long graceful neck. Her waist beneath her exquisite full breasts designed to be fondled, caressed by a man's hand, seemed tiny by comparison. He felt sure he could span it. Her stomach was taut, her hips gently rounded. A tiny patch of black silk veiled her secret core. Her legs were as perfect as any woman's could be. She was the reincarnation of a goddess.

The sense of inevitability was dazzling. He felt a rush of primitive passion he could not fight off. Face drawn, he took hold of her almost fiercely, pulling her with great urgency into the cubicle. There he backed her up against the glass wall, one arm locked tightly around her waist. He used his knee to separate her beautiful legs. The shock of having her naked, trembling flesh against him was so great it might have been mistaken for inner conflict. He could feel the muscles of his face and his body tautening as it came into intimate contact with hers. He could feel his manhood instantly react, swelling with power and desire. She had made it clear she wanted him. Now he would never let her get away.

They were both bathed in steam. Heat rushing inside and

out. His heart pounding, he cupped her moisture-slicked breasts, bent his head to her nipples, flushed with colour. He felt her shudder with rapture as his tongue flicked back and forth, before his mouth came down suckling passionately but with an underlying tenderness he scarcely knew was his gift.

"Jonathon," she cried out, gasping.

"I'm powerless to stop." Now he ground her hips against his as she came up on her toes to accommodate him.

"I don't want you to stop." Her body clung like some wondrous, sinuous vine. "I long for you."

He lost himself then. Lost everything but her. Exultantly he possessed her wet mouth; twining his tongue around hers, thrilled by a depth of passion that matched his own. He let his hands move down over her body, groaning with pleasure at the brush of his hands against her olive, scented flesh. She made him so happy. It was perfect. It was torture. He was deliberately holding back in the tumultuous pursuit of sensation. He wanted to pleasure her as she was delighting him. He wanted to prolong this experience like no other, conscious a tide of excitement was welling higher and higher.

Now suddenly with closed eyes, he placed a finger at the entrance to her vagina. Nothing more. Yet it unleashed a great torrent of emotion. Her moans changed in tone, coming in melting gasps, like she was losing her breath. He wanted to fill her with his driving male lust and his longing, with his love. He wanted to mate with her. He was saturated with excitement. Outside of himself.

"Angel!" He gazed down into her face. Passion had redefined her superb bone structure, the skin so taut she looked chiselled. She was magic! He had no intention of ever letting her get away.

CHAPTER TEN

AT DAWN they melded into each other again. They had spent the night together in Jake's huge king-size bed, making love so glorious the memory of it would never be erased. Later, they were stunned by the revelation they slept wrapped in each other's arms. Not two separate people but close enough for one. Now they re-sought that passionate connection while beyond the verandah, the great symphony of birds brought music to their sexual rapture.

When finally Jake rose to his feet, she put out her arms to entice him back to her side. "Don't go." She wore nothing but the sheet that barely covered her breasts. He could see the deep cleft between them like a smudge of lavender on her olive-ivory skin.

"It's getting late." If he re-entered that bed, he felt he would never get up again.

"Yes. Yes, I know." She sighed voluptuously. "Just sit down for a moment more." She waited then nestled her head beneath his arm to kiss his ribs. "You are the most wonderful lover."

"Good enough to make you stay with me?" He stared down at her. For all their passionate lovemaking, hitherto unimagined or even dreamed of, neither had uttered those momentous words, "I love you."

"It's marvellous here." She continued to kiss his flesh. "I want it always to be like this. You and me. Come back to bed." She moved over enticingly.

He smiled, amber eyes brilliant. There wasn't a trace of tiredness in him for all the experiences of the day before and the fact they'd had little repose. "Don't tempt me," he said very dryly.

"A little longer. I've never known anyone like you." She knelt to cover his shoulders in kisses, her breasts curving in satin globes against his back. "One more time," she sighed.

"You're insatiable!" My God, and he wasn't? "Don't we have a full day?"

She kissed beneath his ear. "I thought time had stood still."

"Angel…" He was weakening, desire rippling into his body on a king tide.

"Tonight then?" she whispered.

"Yes." He pulled her down so her beautiful glossy hair spilled all over her face. "Tomorrow, as well. And the next day. And the next day…" His voice was hypnotic. "I can't get enough of you."

"Kiss me," she begged, aware of the fluttering that had started up in the pit of her stomach and moved to between her legs.

"I shouldn't," he murmured, moving the silky cascade of hair from her face. Nevertheless he risked it.

And was completely lost.

For Angelica the day moved on a high. Nothing went wrong. Nothing could go wrong such was the happiness and optimism of her emotional level. She was in love with the most wonderful man. She believed he loved her, both of them overwhelmed by an experience so divine it was like the gates of heaven had been opened to them, leaving them voiceless with reverence. Even the mercury favoured them, dropping a few degrees though it soared again during the afternoon's play.

The main match, the Marsdon Cup final, was played under brilliantly hot cloudless skies. This didn't appear to deter either players or spectators though the liquid refreshments disappeared at express rate.

The women, looking cool and glamorous, sat on rattan chairs beneath peppermint-striped and fringed umbrellas, slowly sipping long frosted drinks, locked into general conversation and gossip interspersed with cries of bravo and much clapping. The men who weren't playing confined themselves to closely following the match and rehashing their days of glory in the saddle. Polo was the game.

Jake's team, coming in as the underdogs because they had lost one of their best players, was pulling together strongly. On a hunch Jake had substituted Charlie as the Number 1 front player. Charlie, it had to be admitted, had a bit of a wild streak he hadn't yet tamed, but he was a crack horseman and suited to the job of keeping well up the pitch, taking forward passes and shooting for goal.

Both of them, Angelica considered, along with the rest of the female spectators, looked outrageously sexy, the only two golden boys among the dark-haired competitors.

"Charlie's not in love with me, is he?" sighed Gillian, who was looking very chic thanks to a smart new outfit and a little help from Angelica with her hair and make-up. "Why did I ever think he was?"

"Maybe you were in love with love?" Angelica turned lazily to smile at her.

"He's handsome, though, isn't he?"

"He sure is." Angel gave a nod of assent. "He'll be handsomer in a few years."

"You're the one he fancies," Gillian said, surprising her. "He fancied you right off."

"Oh nonsense!" Angel straightened in her rattan chair. "Charlie and I are friendly, that's all. He's very good company, also he was a big help to us." Besides, I'm madly, deeply, wildly in love with your half brother, she omitted to add.

Gillian shrugged that off. "No. I'm not glamorous enough, or exciting enough for Charlie. I'm the girl next door. You're more his style. The truth is I'm far more suited to Ty Caswell. Jake's right."

"To really find out, Gilly, you should do what Charlie's doing. Spread your wings," Angel suggested.

"How exactly?" Gillian eyed her.

"Why not take a job in the city for a while?"

"They'd sack me," Gillian said.

"Why not undertake a course of study? There must be something you'd like to do?"

"I'm not terribly bright, you know," Gillian asserted wryly. "Father was always going on about what a fool I was. He told me I took after Mum. Seems odd, doesn't it, when Jake excelled at everything, academically and on the sports field. All the McCords are clever, influential people. Anyway I don't have to work. Father left me a lot of money. He did it because he had a low opinion of me no doubt."

"It sounds more like he robbed you and your mother of all confidence," Angel said gently. "We'll talk about this some more. Your mother told me she'd like the two of you to visit the cities more. Oh, look, Jake's turned the play back to attack."

"That's why he's the captain," Gillian said smugly. "He's the strongest and best player and he's trained his ponies to be very agile and responsive. They're fast and quick-thinking, too. We should win. That will put Ty's nose out of joint. His team thought they would take it."

Jake's team did win by the narrowest of margins, making for a thrilling, cliffhanger finish. The cup was presented by the wife of one of the biggest property owners in the country—a philanthropist polo devotee—and soon after the grounds cleared as everyone took advantage of the cooling down of late afternoon. The women were all in favour of resting before the expected high jinks of the ball. These functions were known to go right through the night as Outback people extracted every ounce of enjoyment from these legendary weekends.

Coori homestead was crowded with the guests quarters and staff quarters so full that the neighbouring stations helped out with the accommodation. The homestead was looking magnificent and very festive. The splendid tree was such a talking point. They had all worked hard to make sure everything gleamed, sparkled, shone. The flowers, lavish and beautifully

arrange had been flown in, as had seasoned professionals in
the hospitality business, with capabilities well known to
Angelica. The catering, later described in a glossy magazine
as sumptuous, was well in hand.

The Great Hall looked marvellous thanks to Leah's loving,
whimsical, imaginative efforts, but no way could Angelica
get Leah to agree to joining in the social events.

"Better I don't," she told Angelica, not really disap-
pointed. "I've had a great time. Though I couldn't have done
it without you, Miss."

"Just you wait until others can see what you can do,
Leah," Angelica promised. Prophetically as it turned out.

Being in charge of the festivities Angelica had little time
to sit around, though several times she tried it. Her job was
to circulate and see Coori's guests were being well looked
after. With everyone so complimentary, smiles, nods, waves
all 'round, Dinah Campbell emerged the odd woman out.

Dinah let loose her poisonous envy and jealousy the moment she could. It had begun at her first sight of Angelica
standing on the homestead verandah, looking like some film
star in her prime. But since she had caught sight of Angelica
emerging from Jake's room at dawn, wearing only a man's
navy silk robe, her outrage had reached massive proportions.
Who was this woman to push the man she loved from her
life? Dinah burned with anger and humiliation at the utter
unfairness of it. She had survived Jake's other affairs. If she
put her mind to it she could survive this one equally well.

At her first opportunity—it wasn't easy because Miss De
Campo was being made welcome everywhere—Dinah
yielded completely to the jealous ferment that was in her.

"Aren't you a piece of work?" She forcibly steered Angel
away from the crowd with a tight grip on her arm.

"You're too kind." Angelica smiled sweetly as people appeared to be watching their every move. "But please do get
your hand off my arm. I have a brother with a black belt.
He's shown me a few moves."

"God knows you're big enough," Dinah sneered. "Why you wear high heels I'll never know."

They were a distance off, standing beneath the shade of a coolibah, before Dinah released Angelica's arm. "I take it you have a problem?" Angelica eyed the other woman closely, a trifle unnerved by the odd expression in Dinah's eyes, which had turned a livid green.

"I do," Dinah confirmed.

Angelica looked back at the milling crowd. The match was over. Tea, coffee and drinks were still being served in the big marquee. It had been an afternoon of triumph for Coori station. Now this! She wondered whether Dinah was capable of making a scene. She decided she probably was. For all her disdain and general air of superiority Dinah was short on grace. "I only hope you're going to tell me because I have many things left to do." The best part making herself beautiful for Jake.

Dinah looked at her with great contempt. "Like sleeping with Jake? That's right. Don't look away. I saw you sneaking away from his room first thing this morning."

Angelica sighed. "I just knew I couldn't get a clean getaway. Not with you in the house. No wonder you look so jealous." Though she spoke mildly, she was angered by the thought Dinah had been spying on them. "So tell me, what were you doing up at dawn? And at Jake's end of the house? Or don't you need an excuse?"

"Not me!" Dinah glared at her. "You think I haven't been there before?" She flashed Angelica a pitying look. "How could you be such a fool? I've been Jake's girl ever since I can remember. Don't think he's seriously interested in you. What he sees is earthiness. And availability. You exude vulgar sex. You're the one who's been making all the play. Men are permanently unfaithful. Even Jake."

Angelica merely stared at her. "Are you saying this happens in your happy family? I'm sorry. My parents have had a wonderful thirty-year marriage loving only each other. As for Jake, I'd be shocked to know he was promiscuous."

"You know absolutely nothing about Jake," Dinah hissed. "Ever since you arrived you've been working hard to drive him to the limit flaunting that long black hair and your bosom. You've bewitched him if you ask me."

"What would you have me do?" Angelica mocked, secure in the knowledge she had a beautiful body. "Bind my chest down?"

"You might be more modest. You're the kind of woman tailor-made for an affair. Not walking up the aisle. Jake has these affairs from time to time. But he always comes back to me."

"I don't believe that. I can't," Angelica answered quietly, feeling the happiness of the day slipping away.

"No, because you don't want to," Dinah said. "He's dropped all the others. Not me. I'm prepared to hang in there for as long as it takes. As for you! You shared an experience. Fighting the fire together. Jake gave in to lust. That's all it was. You were just an extra service."

"The Bimbo and the Cattle Baron," Angelica mocked. "Forbidden fruit."

"Whatever he does, Jake knows he can come back to me."

"Do you realise you could be wasting your life?" Angelica asked almost kindly.

"I know what I'm about." Dinah's green eyes blazed. "Your little flutter will add up to a great big nothing, you'll see. Try to remember, in a few days' time you go home. And I'll be absolutely ecstatic to see you go."

"Hang on a moment. I believe the family are hoping to see you go first?"

"If you're talking about Stacy and Gillian, they'd better get used to seeing me around. Jake has asked my entire family to the Christmas party, didn't you know?"

"So you figure you can hang around until then?"

"Why not?" Dinah shrugged.

"At least you're thick-skinned," Angelica said. "I wouldn't be too certain if the real lady of the house doesn't politely suggest you buzz off. I think she's had enough of you, but she dislikes unpleasantness.''

"You mean she's a real wimp. Everyone thinks so.''

"You'd better not let Jake hear you say that.''

"As if I would. I'm not a fool, you know.''

"That's a matter of opinion,'' Angelica snapped. "I know exactly what I think of you. Now you must excuse me. It's a shame to waste such a lovely afternoon talking bunkum to you. 'Bye now.''

Dinah's response was to turn on her heel, lips drawn back in a single word. "Bitch!''

It came out quite loudly. Several people turned to stare at her. Some had had a taste of Dinah Campbell's sharp tongue in the past and it still rankled. Good to see the uppity Miss Campbell blow her cool.

By ten o'clock the ball was in full swing. The award-winning band, flown in by charter, played joyously. Everyone was exhilarated and on great form, the women dressed in many bright hues resembled a field of multi-coloured sparkling flowers, smiling radiantly at their men. Leah's billowy cloud ceiling was a great success, the talk of the evening in fact. Guests when they first entered the Great Hall stood in rapt silence to consider it, heads upturned, their expressions filled with pleasure, interest and a measure of surprise. The improvised waterlily lagoon beneath a canopy of trees was rhapsodical, very much suggesting Coori's landscape, inspiring the wealthy philanthropist to remark he could find work for such a talented young lady.

Iridescent dragonflies dipped over the silvered green waters, the magnificent waterlilies painted in their range of colours—pink, white, red, blue, cream—holding their lovely heads above the floating emerald pads. Others admired the floating umbrellas and sporting cups, the way Leah had captured the action of the three polo players, the Number 3 player clearly identifiable as Jake. The whole effect was captivating with considerable technical fluency.

"Gosh, you can even hear the thundering hooves," said Charlie, resplendent in black tie. "Jake looks like a god, doesn't he?" he laughed. He turned to look at Angelica, thinking her a perfect vision. "You look absolutely gorgeous. Tall, slender, beautiful!" He tore his eyes away exclaiming, "That dress! I love it. Did I tell you?"

"At least twice." Angelica smiled, laying a hand on his jacketed arm. "But I don't mind hearing it again."

"This is grand." Charlie was determined to make a night of it. "What I'd really like is to dance. Game?"

"I'd love it!" Angelica answered promptly.

Charlie led her out onto the floor chortling. He'd dreamed of having a flutter with a magnificent female. Maybe he might finally get lucky. His two-year stint on a great Australian cattle station had been an adventure. He didn't believe he would ever forget it. But he accepted he would be going home. One day, like Jake, whom he admired enormously, he would have to take his father's place. But for now? Angelica was smiling at him and her big beautiful dark eyes looked so inviting. She was without question the most beautiful woman in the room. And the most exciting. His sense of adventure was at work again!

Standing in the middle of a crowd of friends, Jake saw them take the floor. They looked spectacular. Charlie, off duty, dressed in a dinner jacket, was every inch the Honourable Charles Middleton. And he had such a great zest for life. Not that it hadn't gotten him into his fair share of trouble. No one could miss the fact either that Charlie found Angel a real knockout. His expression, which he didn't bother to hide, was a dead give-away. Much as he liked Charlie, Jake was startled to discover he didn't like the way Charlie had Angel locked in his arms. Charlie, frankly, looked in seventh heaven. Angel looked what? Indulgent? The two of them got on well. Ah well, enjoy yourself for the time being, Charlie, Jake thought silently. That woman is mine.

It was hard to listen to what the senator was saying when

he couldn't take his eyes off them. Angel was wearing the most beautiful dress he'd ever seen and there were some stunning dresses out there on the dance floor. The young women in particular, just loved these social occasions as it gave them the opportunity to dress up. Everyone made sure they looked their very best, going all out on the gowns. Gillian in a deep pink strapless organza dress with a skirt that looked like petals had never looked prettier. Stacy, too, had done him proud in sequined blue that showed off her youthful petite figure. But Angel. Wow!

How to describe that dress? It was very, very sexy and very imaginative. Not like the usual evening dress at all but a creation in gold, silver and sage green with ribbons and all kinds of fancy beadwork and sequins. A man could never describe it. The slip bodice was low-cut, revealing the swell of her beautiful breasts, the skirt had a deep flounce that showed a lot of leg. She looked like a film star. God, yes! Charlie thought so, too. He'd go and cut in just as soon as the senator stopped talking.

Charlie was a fast worker. Challenge dictated his every move. Not that Charlie knew anything about his involvement with Angel. Neither of them had put their feelings on display. Rather the reverse. Charlie was light-footed, light-hearted. Angel appeared to be floating... Hell, Charlie was tap dancing!

"...so in the end it was my lucky night!" the senator concluded, while they all laughed heartily.

Dinah, in emerald-green silk satin, her platinum hair artfully tousled, laughed, too, though her gaze had long since shifted away from the senator to follow Jake's. That woman with too much of her body on display was dancing with Charles Middleton! Surely that wasn't cracking Jake up? She was hardly the solid, faithful type.

And didn't Charles look polished. Unrecognisable, really, from the station jackeroo. Not that he'd ever been treated like one. As far as she knew Gilly had had a crush on Charles. That was a cause for amusement. Not that one could blame the poor little thing, though she did look remarkably glamorous tonight. Stacy did, too.

It was getting tiresome, Miss De Campo's interference. Apparently she had helped them achieve what they had never achieved before. An appearance in line with the McCord family status. Stacy had sprung another surprise getting it together with Leif Standford, the financier, who owned a string of winning race horses. Leif, a widower, would eventually remarry, but Dinah would never have thought ineffectual little Stacy would take his eye. Yet they'd been glued to one another's side all night. Extraordinary!

To top it off, Charles, it now appeared, was very interested in the dark-eyed, dark-haired Miss De Campo's anatomy, if nothing else. Unless she was very much mistaken, Jake didn't like it at all. His golden eyes might look lazy beneath his marked, bronze brows, he had a smile on his beautiful mouth, but she knew Jake. He was watching Charles and the Mediterranean sex goddess like the proverbial hawk. Surely this was a god-sent opportunity to do a little mischief? Jake really should see that woman for what she was. Specifically, a tart. There must be some way to work it, to push Charles and Miss De Campo together.

This was a party, after all, and there was plenty of alcohol. The last time she'd seen Charles at one of these do's he'd been quite frenetic. What she had in mind was a dawn orgy. Her Jake wouldn't be happy about that. Well now it was payback time! Revenge was her middle name.

Charles handed Angelica over without demur. ''That was great, Angelica!'' he said, laughing into her beautiful, black-lashed eyes. ''Now the boss is here, I'll have to hand you over.''

''Goodbye, Charlie,'' Jake drawled. ''Stay away.''

''I'll be back!'' Charlie grinned boldly.

''I feel I can't let you out of my sight,'' Jake muttered, gathering her hungrily close. It was an action that plunged them into passionate intimacy.

''Sounds fine to me,'' Angelica answered huskily. She'd

been having fun with the debonair Charlie, but she'd been longing for the moment when Jake would cross the room and take her into his arms. He wore a white dinner jacket and the effect against his tawny colouring and golden-bronze skin was startlingly attractive. He was a powerfully sexual man yet he seemed quite unaware of it and his extraordinary looks.

''Watch Charlie,'' he said, with an unconscious little edge.

She drew back a little to stare into his amber eyes. ''Don't you trust me?''

''I don't trust Charlie,'' he told her dryly. ''When Charlie gets a mad idea into his head he takes off. He's extremely impulsive.''

''Why he's a few years younger than I am,'' she pointed out in amazement. Indeed she thought of Charlie as still a boy.

''Sure,'' he softly jeered, ''and I'm thinking he's getting carried away.''

''Good thinking on your part.'' She had to laugh, aware of Charlie's youthful interest. ''I can handle Charles.''

''I'm glad to hear it.''

''He's only having fun. You don't think you're a little bit jealous?'' Looking into his eyes gave her enormous pleasure.

''I can promise I will be. I don't want anyone to put their arms around you but me.'' The whole truth and nothing but the truth.

''I love that.'' She sighed and flushed like a rose. It was such rapture to be in his arms. Every cell in her body reacted.

''I adore that dress. It's beautiful. The only thing I'd like more is to peel it off you.''

The sensuality in his voice made her tremble. ''I'm going to let you.'' She raised her huge dark eyes to him.

They were made desperately lovely because of some shadow she wore on the lids, a mysterious green like her dress. Had he really made endless love to her? Made her come over and over or had he only dreamt it? He would have died for a kiss at that moment, his desire for her so powerful

he was almost afraid of it. He hadn't thought himself such a
vulnerable man. But he was where she was concerned.
Without even trying she attracted every male within range.
It was a power she had and that power, he knew, wouldn't
cease. She'd probably have it when she was an old lady. The
man who married her would have to be prepared for fighting
off all comers even if she was a woman of unquestioned
loyalty. He was in love with her. Within days in fact of asking her to marry him. If she said yes, could there be a better
Christmas?

"What would I do if you went away?" he mused aloud.

"I'm not leaving." She intended it to sound like a little
joke, instead her voice betrayed her. It was intense and emotional. Why? She loved him.

"I just cannot believe this has all happened so quickly,"
he said, smoothing his cheek against her glossy hair.

"But what a miracle!" she breathed.

Across the Great Hall Dinah watched them with a cold
weight on her heart. She had never seen Jake like this before.
Not with anyone. He'd gone overboard for this woman, who
had to be really clever. Well, she could be clever, too. Certain
things she knew Jake hated. Unfaithfulness was one of them.
She remembered his outburst when their friends, the
Hammonds, broke up. They'd all suspected Lucienne had
been having an affair. Jake hadn't liked that one little bit.
Jake liked to think marriage was forever.

It was easy for Dinah to get Charles to dance with her.
Better yet, she thought he was a little drunk, though his
movements were controlled enough. "I saw you dancing
with Miss De Campo," she said archly, cocking her platinum
head to one side. "Now there's a swinger. A real party-party
girl, if you know what I mean?"

"I adore her," said Charles, thinking he had never suc-
ceeded in liking Jake's ex-girlfriend, Dinah Campbell. So
what if she was good-looking and her family was supposed
to be loaded? There was a hardness behind the expensive

wrapping and those pretty, cool green eyes. Frankly he didn't think she was good enough for Jake.

"And she likes you," Dinah continued, playing him as though he were a simple child. "She finds you thoroughly attractive, sophisticated and worldly. Not difficult to see why. You look marvellous in black tie, and of course you are the Honourable Charles Middleton. It shows."

If only she weren't such an embarrassing snob!

"You've made quite an impression on her."

For a moment Charles was quite overcome. That beautiful woman attracted to him? That was a huge coup. It stunned him. "How do you know?" he demanded, maddened he hadn't had a clue.

"Why she told me, obviously," Dinah trilled. "I'm sure she'd be yours if you want."

Charles wanted badly. Man was born to sow his wild oats! Supper came and went though it was more like a banquet. The buffet tables were laden with the most delectable food including ham, turkey, chicken, beef, served in hot or cold dishes. Magnificent seafood had been flown in from tropical North Queensland—lobster, crab, the Gulf's famous prawns, oysters nestling in ice; pasta dishes, all kinds of salads. There was a separate buffet table for the splendid desserts. Waiters circled constantly, refilling champagne flutes. It couldn't have been more splendid or more festive. Christmas was definitely in the air.

It was around two in the morning when that daredevil Charles suggested a treasure hunt. Treasure hunts went off very well at home and they did offer distinct romantic possibilities. It was a huge inducement to know Angelica was attracted to him. After all, he had plenty to offer. The younger guests received the suggestion with much clapping and cheering.

The boundaries were set and included the avenues of walkways connecting the Great Hall with the homestead as well as the Great Hall and its immediate grounds. The homestead itself was off limits. The treasure was to be planted by Jake, as master of Coori station and their host.

Once Jake moved off—he was given ten minutes to find a suitable hiding place—Charlie seized Angelica's hand. "You're with me," he said, flushed with triumph. "Jake can't be in the game. He knows where the treasure's hidden."

His mood was infectious. Though Charlie was almost an adolescent, he was good fun. Out under the stars they heard peals of giggles; girl's voices, light, sweet and young. The black-velvet sky was ribboned by the Milky Way, a glorious diamond haze containing billions of stars.

It was utterly beautiful! Angelica looked up, marking the stars that made up the constellation of the Southern Cross. It hung over the homestead's great roof, easy to pick out in the pure desert air. The star furthest to the south was a star of the first magnitude. East and north, the second magnitude. To the west, a star of the third magnitude. In ancient times it was visible in Babylonia and Greece.

"You're not supposed to be star-gazing," Charlie whispered in her ear, his excitement gathering by the moment. "We're looking for treasure. Or we're supposed to be." He wondered wildly if he should kiss her now. But just as he thought it, he had to think again. Another couple followed them up.

"You behave yourself, Charlie," said the guy, one of the members of the opposing polo team.

"Isn't that what I always do," Charlie quipped, leading Angelica across the springy grass to one of the vine-covered bowers, its flowers glowing radiantly.

"I'm not sure Jake would plant it here." She smiled, not much caring. The breeze was glorious, carrying the marvellous perfume of the purple boronia that grew wild. It was a fantastic night. She was so happy! Her thoughts were entirely of Jake. Not of Charlie, greatly misled.

For a while Charlie made a pretence of looking for the treasure, shaking out plants and looking around and beneath all the stone garden benches. They were moving further away from the lights that blazed around the Great Hall. The home gardens had been lit for the occasion, a veritable fairyland, but there were delicious pockets of dark.

Finally Charlie couldn't stand it. He stood stock-still, staring down into Angelica's pearlescent face. It took a special kind of man to lead a celibate life. It was not a life for him!

"What then?" she whispered, wondering why he had stopped.

"Oh, Angelica, why didn't you tell me you were attracted to me?" he asked tenderly.

That brought Angelica back to earth with a crash. "Charlie," she exhaled in shock, "I'm not attracted to you."

But heat was flowing into Charlie at the rate of knots. He put his hands on her shoulders, revelling in the feel of her bones and her satiny, perfumed skin. "You don't mean that." Not since Dinah's revelation.

"I absolutely do." She tried to sound stern and failed. "If you don't stop being silly, I'm going back."

But Charlie, intoxicated on all fronts, was under a pounding, painful desire. God knows, he didn't get to meet too many beautiful women miles way out in the bush. "You can't!" he protested in a spectacularly loud voice.

"Shh, be quiet!" Embarrassed, Angel looked back over her shoulder.

"No. Angelica, there's a good side to this," he informed her.

"Really, what?"

"I can afford to come to Sydney to see you. I could spend some time in the New Year with you."

"Oh, Charlie, no more!" Angel pleaded, unwilling to hurt his feelings. "You're being ridiculous. I've never given you the slightest encouragement. Not now. Not ever. I think you've had a bit too much to drink. We really ought to go back."

"Not until I've kissed you," Charlie said masterfully. It had always worked with Gilly. With a smooth slide of muscle he hauled her up against him, kissing her frantically though she tried to jerk her head back.

"You're beautiful, so beautiful!" His young voice literally shook with excitement. "You wanted that, didn't you?"

What she really wanted to do was sock him, her long hair thrashing from side to side as she attempted to wrestle him off. "Charlie, stop this," she gritted. "Someone will come along."

"Let them. Oh, hell, Angelica, did you have to kick me?" Charlie broke off to press his hand against his shin. "The truth is I'm mad about you. I just realised it. Dinah Campbell tipped me off."

"Dinah Campbell?" Angelica felt a red tide of anger as Charlie straightened, locking a finger around her wrist.

"Yes, Dinah," he confided. "I don't like her much but she did me a favour." Charlie, with a huge capacity for pleasure, reached for her again, holding her face still in his hands while he planted an emotion-charged kiss on her mouth. "I'll do the right thing by you," he muttered when he was able to talk at all.

"Hey, don't worry!" Angelica kicked him again and Charlie gave a moan of pain, perceiving through an alcohol-induced fog, Dinah, sinister sort of girl that she was, might have led him astray. Angelica didn't appear to be keen on him after all. "Don't be like this," he coaxed. "Really, Dinah's the one who should be shot. The bitch! I'm so sorry. I was out of line. Let's kiss and make up." He risked placing an arm around her, bending his blond head. He wanted to steal a kiss one last time!

Simultaneously Jake found them, silhouetted against nearby lights. Which was exactly what Dinah had planned on. To all appearances they were locked in each other's arms, enjoying a smouldering kiss. Angel's long hair was cascading down her back. One shoulder was entirely bare, as the thin strap of her gown slid down her arm, revealing more of her breast. Her skin glowed in the semi-dark.

He went to earth with his deepest emotions. He realised

he'd always lived that way. He wondered briefly if she were a nymphomaniac, and quickly rejected it disgustedly as part of the jealousy process. More likely men couldn't keep their hands off her. Either way it would be hell to be married to her.

Blessed with excellent night vision he stared for a long while hoping with all his heart Angel when released would reach back and slap Charlie's handsome face. She didn't. Instead they spoke quietly for a moment, dark and fair heads together as though planning another assignation. Then Angel turned away no doubt to return to the Hall. And she was going alone. Charlie, just like in a movie, skulked off in the opposite direction.

Head down, moving so innocently in her exquisite seductive gown, she almost walked into him. "Jake!" She clutched her throat. She seemed guilty, as though caught in the act.

"Have you ever tried getting treatment?" he asked acidly, knowing full well pain was making him lash out even as it heightened his desire.

She placed a gentle, restraining hand on his arm. "Charlie is drunk," she explained, much as she might say little Kylee was being naughty. "You know what he's like. He lost it for a while."

"You mean another one went off the deep end?" It sounded brutal. He didn't want that, but he was injured.

"Men being what they are," she said with hurt sarcasm. "Look, I like Charlie. He's just a boy."

"Some boy!" he responded tight-lipped, wanting to crush her mouth under his. The problem was he was too proud. And so afraid of loving. He abandoned himself to jealous rage, doubly angry because he had never really experienced the emotion before. In fact he was in awe of it. He had never depended on anyone outside his beloved mother for emotional support, until he met this woman. "So far as I could see he had his tongue down your throat," he bit off. Even as he said it he felt wretched.

"How would you know? Have you got X-ray vision?"

she challenged him, her own temper rising though she
scented his hard desire.

"You're damned right I have. What did you go with him
for anyway?"

"You want to forbid me to walk with anyone else?" She
leaned towards him as though he, not Charlie, would be the
recipient of a good back-hander.

"I think I told you to watch out for Charlie," he said
harshly.

"That's me, a siren, luring men onto the rocks. Can't you
trust me for five minutes, Jonathon?"

He took a deep breath, feeling it shake in his throat. "God
knows I want to." Why couldn't he say, "I love you"? Or
was he going to be trapped forever? "I thought we had something valuable," he said. "Something important. Something
that would lead us to make vows. But for God's sake, do
you have to lead every man in sight into temptation?" He
knew he should stop but he couldn't, enwrapped in a lifetime
of bitter disappointments.

Her beautiful face registered anger and pain. "Of course I
do!" She gave another angry laugh. "It's never the man's
fault, is it? I'd have a lifetime of getting the blame from you
if we were married."

"Oh, so you thought I was going to ask you to marry
me?" he asked with a touch of his father's cruelty. It sounded
like an obscenity in his own ears.

"Weren't you?" she seethed. "Or was I just another one
of your affairs? Dinah told me you had them from time to
time. She also told poor alcohol-impaired Charlie that I had
the hots for him. Or words to that effect."

"Dinah did?" He felt sick. Like he'd done some irrepa-
rable damage by rushing into judgment when she could simply be telling the truth.

"That's right. Are you surprised? Dinah, your friend," she
said fiercely. "She wanted to discredit me. And she knows
all about you. More than I do, at any rate. She knows what
a puritan you are. The worse kind of man. Like your father."

A stricken silence. "I didn't mean that." Her voice shook. "You make me so angry, but I didn't mean it."

"Maybe you're right," he said, his grave face poised above her. "There are certain things I want from the woman I'd ask to be my wife. I thought I'd met her. I don't count Charlie. I understand what stage Charlie's at. But I meant nothing to you. You could have stopped him. Charlie might be a bit drunk but he's not the kind to force a woman."

"Really? I thought you were all that kind," she returned cuttingly, pain clawing at her. "The world could drown in a woman's tears. You're a long way from being my ideal man, Jonathon McCord. In fact, I don't want you to ever speak to me again. Except on business." With that, she gathered her long skirt with one hand and started to stalk off, turning abruptly to warn, "And if you say one more nasty word about me, I'm going to sue you for defamation of character. I'll tell Bruno, as well, though he mightn't have as easy a time knocking you flat like he did Trevor. I don't give men a great big come-on, as you desperately want to believe. I don't think you'll ever get over losing your mother. Loving comes with punishment in your book. In a good marriage— and I know because my parents have one—there's trust on both sides. It's time you learned something about it. Good night!"

He went after her, stung insufferably by her little speech. "Don't you dare go to bed." When he desperately wanted her there. "You're working, remember?" Hell, how stupid, but there didn't seem to be a way around this pain.

"I think I'll hand over to Stacy if you don't mind."

The fact her cheek glistened with a tear came as a near physical blow to his heart. "God, Angel, I'm sorry." His anger totally collapsed, revealing his very real love for her. "I'm sure you're right in everything you say. It's me, not you. I had a terrible childhood and it's made me hard. Wanting you is something over which I have no control, when control has always been my thing."

"I don't think you could ever change." She bit her lip, dreadfully upset.

"I love you." The words burst forth, though they seemed to give her no satisfaction. "I hoped you loved me. I thought what we had was perfect."

"Nothing's perfect, Jonathon." She sighed shakily and turned away.

CHAPTER ELEVEN

By MID-AFTERNOON of the following day the guests with the exception of Dinah Campbell and Leif Standford had returned home. He'd realised for some time his stepmother had a soft spot for Leif and that was one of the reasons he'd been invited to the match. Now it seemed Leif returned Stacy's affections. He hoped the friendship would progress. God knows, Stacy had had little marital happiness. Leif was a good man.

As for Dinah, he planned a quiet talk with her, stung with distaste for what she had attempted to do. Charlie could get himself into enough trouble without anyone's help. Not that he was worried about Charlie. Charlie would always fall on his feet. He was more worried about himself.

It seemed a dreadful thing now he had expected the worst of Angel, then throw it at her. He had never been like this before. He had never been head over heels in love before. He had never had so many struggles going on in his head and body. He'd seen her only once that day, so vividly darkly beautiful she made the breath catch in his throat. She showed no signs of the upset of the night before, or the fact she'd probably only had an hour or two's sleep. She'd said a polite, "Good morning," and gone on her way. It shook him up a little but there were too many distractions. Guests had to be ferried to the airstrip, fare-welled. Everyone agreed it was the best day ever. Or at least until next year, though Angel's efforts would be very hard indeed to top. Not in his experience anyway.

"If I were you, son," the senator told him confidentially, grasping him by the shoulder, "I'd marry that girl. She's everything you're going to need in a wife. We have high hopes for you politically.''

It wasn't the first time he'd heard it and his general thoughts had been at some stage he might be able to do some good for the man on the land. But Angel? He could never allow her to end the relationship if he had to go down on his bended knee and beg forgiveness.

He caught up with Dinah as she was walking back to the homestead after a stroll in the home gardens. He was determined to have it out. She gave him a bright smile and a wide-eyed-innocent look.

''Thank goodness they've all gone,'' she said, as if they were in perfect agreement, ''though we did have a marvellous night.''

''You certainly did trying to spread mischief.'' He came out with it, directly watching her smile disappear.

''She told you,'' she said flatly, colour staining her cheeks.

''Yes, she did. Seeing her in his arms made me crazy just like you intended. Charlie knows nothing about Angel and me.''

''And what about Angelica and you?'' Dinah spat.

''I love her,'' he said simply. ''I loved her the moment I set eyes on her.''

''You lusted after her, don't you think?'' she retorted with great bitterness.

''That, too. A man lusts after his woman. But I want her heart and her mind. I want all of her.''

''God knows there's enough,'' she said roughly, tormenting herself with what might have been.

Jake looked away from her and her naked jealousy, unhappy it had come this far. ''I've never wanted to hurt you, Dinah. I made you no promises. What we had wasn't near enough for commitment. You'll find someone else if you can fight out of your obsession with being mistress of Coori. You want the house as much as me. Don't you think I've seen you looking at it?''

''Because I could do so much with it,'' she said strongly.

"I'm right for you, Jake. Can't you see that? I've loved you all my life. She'll give you hell."

He laughed sharply. "Even if she did it would be worth it, but Angelica is a good woman. I'm the one with the demon. You met him. He was my dad."

"Your father approved of me," she reminded him. "He wanted us to get married."

He nodded, his deep-seated anger and resentment of his late father finally spent. "That's so, Dinah, but Dad's gone for good. You mightn't think it now, but we'd have been miserable together."

"Not true, Jake," she protested, touching her fingers to her eyelids to suppress the pain that was starting up, "I love you."

"If you do, it hasn't made either of us happy," Jake murmured quietly. "I'm sorry, Dinah. My advice to you is to go home. I don't want you to stay on for the Christmas party. I figure we can have the house to ourselves for a change. I've seen you patronising my stepmother and my sister. I've never liked it. They don't like it, either."

"But I will see you at Christmas?" she pleaded, seemingly unable to accept rejection.

"It might be better if you don't," he answered. "I'm going to ask Angel to marry me. I want her to forgive me for being such a fool."

Finally the magnitude of her mistake got through to her. Face flaming, Dinah turned away, making for the house to pack her luggage. "You are a fool," she burst out explosively over her shoulder. "And I hate you both. She's going to lead you a merry dance. She'll drive you up the wall."

"I'll get used to it. Believe me!" He heard himself laughing. It felt wonderful. Liberating. Now he had to make his peace with Angel. He'd better make it good.

Dinah, storming into the house, was confronted by the sight of the woman she now hated with a passion. She was stacking even more presents under the towering Christmas tree, her face full of a nauseating maternal tenderness. Quite

the Madonna. Dinah, an arch conservative, still thought the
Christmas tree would have looked better put to one side, not
dominating the entrance hall with its gaudiness and overkill.
Just like Miss De Campo herself. With her, apparently the
object of her affection, was the aboriginal child Kylee, with
the big black eyes, the tousled ginger curls and the woefully
cheeky tongue. She was gleefully sitting among the pile of
expensively wrapped boxes pulling at a spectacular red-and-
gold decoration atop one box.

"Leave that alone," Dinah called out sharply, wishing
Jake had never laid eyes on this woman. She could have hung
in there and become mistress of this house. She could have
put everyone and everything straight. She could have been
such an asset to Jake. She had the right sort of backbone.

They both turned to stare at her. Woman and child. "Go
away, lady," the child piped up.

Angelica shook her head quickly. "No, Kylee. Be a good
girl now."

"As if she'd know how! And you encourage her." Dinah
dissolved into a sick rage. "You don't know anything about
the way we do things around here. That child has no place
in the house. She should be with her mother. She's the house
girl, isn't she? A domestic."

"Well, yes, that's the way you see things, Dinah,"
Angelica said. "I don't. By the way, your plan nearly suc-
ceeded last night."

Dinah's eyes appraised her with hatred. "I know. I've been
speaking to Jake. He's disgusted with you."

"Disgusted with himself more like it!" Jake appeared in
the open doorway, staring across at Angelica for a long moment, his repentant heart in his amber eyes. "It's time you
left Coori, Dinah," he advised, almost kindly. "I'm in love
with Angelica. She's the only woman for me."

"You'll be sorry, Jake," Dinah warned, a crazy energy
building up in her. Finally she cracked, hopelessness and humiliation taking its toll. She looked around wildly for something to throw. Something to break. Her hand closed on one

of a pair of bronze winged figures. She threw it wildly, not at Jake, but at Angelica, who had wrecked all their lives.

With excellent reflexes, Angelica bent sideways sheltering Kylee with her body. The statue crashed into the Christmas tree, dislodging several ornaments and breaking a porcelain cupid.

"See what you done!" Kylee cried, already scrambling to her feet. "You're a nasty lady!" she squealed, bursting into tears.

Angelica levered herself up, watching Dinah fly up the stairs. "Go after her, Jonathon. She can't fly anywhere in that condition."

"Are you giving me orders?" He spun to face her, heartened beyond words she had called him Jonathon.

"Yes I am. You said you love me, goddamn it!"

"You drive me crazy nearly as much," he retorted, revelling in her response.

"Luv, luv!" Excitedly, Kylee started to dance, waving her little arms and twisting her knees like the natural dancer she was. "All we need is luv!" she shouted.

"Kylee's got the right idea." Jake strode to Angelica, pulling her to her feet. "I love you. Love you. Love you," he breathed. "You're my every want. My every need. I want you to marry me," he whispered in her ear. "I know this isn't the right moment. I'm going to ask you again later."

"What makes you think I'm going to say yes?" She stretched out a gentle hand to touch his face.

"We'll see." He looked down at her so thrillingly it evoked mental pictures of the two of them in his great bed, locked in each other's arms.

"Am I going to get a present for Christmas, Mr. Jake?" Kylee stopped gyrating long enough to ask.

"Sure you are, sweetheart." He reached out to muss her curls. "I'm going to send you a Christmas present every year. Wherever you are." A promise he was destined to keep.

"Oh, great!" Kylee was overwhelmed with joy, showing it in her smiling little face. "I love Christmas. I love the little

Christ child. I love Mary and Joseph and the manger. I love Mummy and you and Miss. And oh yes, Clary. She's always got something nice for me.''

"And I'll have something nice for you," Jake murmured for Angelica alone. "Only you. Only you."

To Kylee's absolute delight Mr. Jake kissed Miss. It was a lovely long kiss that went on and on. Both of them had their eyes closed.

Exactly a year later they had their first baby. They called her Noelle. She was utterly adored. She had her father's amber locks and right from the beginning her mother's melting dark eyes.

As for Jonathon and Angelica?

Each new day filled them with fresh wonder. Coori station was once more a happy place.

All it took was an angel.